LEGACY OF AN IMMIGRANT

"This book is an unusual combination of storytelling and historical events, as seen through the eyes of a thirteen-year-old, Eugene. The story rotates around the funeral of a beloved grandfather, Caesar Lucchesi, and his love for flying. However, there is a deeper feature to the book. The understanding and acceptance of death are conceptual processes that lead us into the unknown singular territory of ourselves. As Eugene's Uncle Geno says, 'death and grief are hard to understand.'"
— Kathleen Johnson, PhD Theology, Hospice Chaplain

"In *Legacy of an Immigrant: Four Generations of Flying*, Maria Vezzetti Matson gives young readers a framework to see their dreams develop from influence and inspiration to achievement through a story of family and loss. Young readers interested in aviation and history will be captivated and motivated by this story."
— Anders Hill, Superintendent, Houghton-Portage Township Schools

"I grew up down the block from the Vezzettis and know the family in this book very well! Seven years younger than Eugene, I also found myself flying for a career, first as a naval aviator and then for Delta in Boeing Aircraft. *Legacy of an Immigrant* is a remarkable story of the shared love of a grandfather and grandson. Both aviators touched history with their achievements in the sky!"
— Captain Marc Caspary, Delta Airlines (ret.), Naval Aviator (ret.)

Legacy of an Immigrant: Four Generations of Flying

Published by:
Polenta Publishing
P.O. Box 954
Glen Ellen, California, 95442

Address all inquiries to:
Maria Vezzetti Matson
mariavmatson@gmail.com

www.MariaVezzettiMatsonAuthor.com

Disclaimer.
This book is a work of fiction. The story is inspired by the aviation history of the author's family. All of the people in the story either are made up or real. Any resemblance to living or deceased people should be obvious to them and others who know them, especially if the author has been gracious enough to reveal their actual names. All historical events depicted there occurred, albeit the author has taken liberties with some details on occasion. I mean no harm.

ISBN: 978-0-9831990-5-2
Library of Congress Control Number: 2022913546

Editor: Tyler Tichelaar, Superior Book Productions
Cover and Interior Design: Smythtype Design

Interior art credits:
NPS, Keweenaw NHP, Lucchesi family papers, Saint Louis Air Races [program]
    pp. 31 & 33, 1937
dosunsets/iStock, pp. 11, 19, 101

Every attempt has been made to properly source all quotes.

For additional copies, contact:
www.MariaVezzettiMatsonAuthor.com

Printed in the United States of America
First Edition
2 4 6 8 10 12

LEGACY OF AN IMMIGRANT

Four Generations of Flying

A Novel

Maria Vezzetti Matson

To all aviators and aspiring pilots.

Preface

A health concern sparked the motivation for this story. I was scared that during the summer of 2020, my elder brother would be infected with the COVID-19 virus and die. My apprehensions were not unwarranted. The COVID pandemic killed a significant number of people all across the world. Our family's aviation memories, particularly my brother's participation in the 75th anniversary of Normandy's D-Day in 2019, deserved to be recorded and shared. Some personalities in this story are made up, but many settings and names are accurate.

Aside from flying, the story also deals with the death of a grandparent. In 1957, Eugene was thirteen years old when his grandfather, The Boss, Caesar Lucchesi, died. At the end of the book, I have included some discussion questions that you might find helpful in tackling the issue of sorrow. While reading, I hope the story motivates you to laugh, cry, learn, and take the time to tell someone you love them.

Contents

Part I
July 2020

AUTHOR'S NOTES

Greetings—may I have your attention? On behalf of Polenta Publishing, it is my pleasure to welcome all readers aboard.

Prior to continuing, the author wishes to share some important features of this story.

Use caution when reading this novel—all stories have three sides: yours, mine, and the truth.

You may proceed into Part I and return to this information below or continue reading and take note of the author's use of truth and fiction.

ALERT Fact or Fiction *ALERT*

Please, take a moment to review some of the facts as you read.

The following items are authentic: the protagonist Eugene, his career facts, and his participation in the 75th D-Day Anniversary. His grandfather, Caesar, was a pioneering regional aviator, too. The setting, location names, and Lucy the dog are accurate. Unfortunately, so is the COVID-19 pandemic.

Keep in mind that written within the facts is fiction: the grandchildren, the interviewer, and the interview are for your reading pleasure.

The author hopes that blending fact and fiction makes for a smooth and first-class read. Please take a moment to make sure your seat belts are fastened. Now, prepare for takeoff. Enjoy your journey into *The Legacy of an Immigrant.*

"Truth is stranger than fiction. It has to be!
Fiction has to be possible and truth doesn't!"

— Mark Twain

Chapter 1

The phone goes off like there is a five-alarm fire. It never stops. "Could someone please answer the phone?" Nobody responds to me. I am shouting into a silent kitchen.

The annoying noise comes from beneath a newspaper. I focus on the papers, thinking my wicked gaze will silence the sounds. It doesn't work, so I move the *Daily Mining Gazette* and answer. An unknown voice says my name.

"Maybe this is Eugene speaking. Why do you want to speak to him? Who is this?"

The caller begins to tell me why they are calling but not who they are.

"I'm writing a summer school paper about your family's flying past beginning with your grandfather, Mr. Lucchesi. He flew during the Golden Age of Aviation, and it is a story worth telling. He was your grandfather, correct?"

I'm unsure whether the voice is that of a girl or young boy, but I am sure of my grandfather's background.

"Yes, Caesar Lucchesi was my grandfather. Why are you interested in my grandfather's early flying days? Who is this?" The youthful voice on the opposite end insists it will be a short call. My question about their name goes unanswered. The youngster on the other end is polite, and I am intrigued by the caller's approach.

I spy two of my grandchildren outside waving for my attention through the kitchen window. It takes my attention away from my call. I'm not too concerned because the two cousins are in their teens and old enough to take care of themselves for a bit.

"What?" I pause. "You're right about how my grandfather and I flew at the Sands airport. I got lucky." They correct me for using the word lucky. "Oh, you prefer me to use the word fortunate instead of lucky?"

That is a bit strange—this phone call is becoming crazy. I pause to listen as the caller rattles off names and dates like a robot. Someone did their homework before calling me. "Yes, they're my uncles. Uncle Geno indeed ran the aviation school. Yup, his brother Fred was a mechanic. Who told you all of that?"

The caller names their source, but it means nothing to me. My gaze is drawn again to the youngsters along the waterway's shores. "So you had a relative who knew my relatives. Okay, so why do you need to talk to me? I only have a few minutes because I have grandkids outside needing my attention."

The strange phone conversation becomes weirder. They know lots of personal stuff about my grandfather's life. The next question makes me squirm, and I shuffle from foot to foot. I want to hang up now.

The voice on the opposite end of the line asks, "Tell me how you felt on September 7, 1957, at your grandfather's burial."

"Umm, Caesar's funeral? Yes, you've got the date right. I do remember that day, but I'm not sure you need to know how I felt."

I remind myself to be cautious about what I share. A guy like me likes to talk about facts, not emotions. I am not particularly eager to relive that day. And not in the mood to talk about my feelings with a stranger.

"I don't like telling you personal info," is my delayed answer. Clearing my throat, I begin again. "Yes, I'm still on the line. You surprised me with your question. Caesar died in 1957. You don't expect me to remember everything—that's so long ago. I was a kid and only thirteen years old. Now it's 2020. I'm too busy worrying about COVID-19 to be thinking about the past right now."

I have no intention of discussing my sorrows with an unknown individual. It is time to hang up, but I keep talking. The voice on the phone begins to speak, interrupting me.

"Please repeat it. Yes, you hit the nail on the head; I am seventy-six. Yes, aviation has played a major role throughout my life. The third generation of flyers, to be exact. Right again. Last year, I participated in the Daks over Normandy D-Day events. How did you, umm?" Once again, the persistent caller won't let me finish. I keep my mouth shut and wait until a pause occurs.

"Is your dream to be a pilot like me?"

The student caller corrects me.

"Oh, not a pilot but an...."

The answer I hear makes me grin. My grandkids know my love of history and must be playing a prank on me with this call. The kids set this up and fed the caller all this information. Yes, the kids knew I lived with my grandparents when I was a child. Yes, everyone knows I am a Michigan Tech graduate. I am positive the phone call is a hoax the kids planned.

Okay, I'll go along with it and get my revenge later. My three clever grandchildren and I are always trying to outwit each other with trickery. My mind wanders to a payback scheme, and I ask, "Do you know anything about my first job?"

The speaker takes a breather. I imagine them going over notes written by my sassy grandkids.

The grandkids have no idea how I got to work with a specific flying firm by using the Lucchesi name. Working with the company was sensible and, also, stupid. Their flight hours gave me credibility on my resume for my next job, but I worked there without pay. It was free labor for the flying company. The caller interrupts me. Their awareness of my work experience makes me nervous.

"Oh, so you do know about the Iron Mountain work? Now,

tell me, who put you up to this? Am I on a reality television show?" I shuffle books on a shelf, looking for a concealed camera inside the house. "Yes, my first paid job involved the delivery of mail and freight."

The back door shuts, capturing my attention. Angelina, my eldest granddaughter, and her dog walk into the house. She is a jogger who just returned from a run. Removing the face mask, she places it on the table and hums a tune. Angelina tosses her long dark hair from side to side while the dog circles her. She is the eldest of the three cousins who reunite with me each summer in Michigan.

"What's there to eat?" The refrigerator door opens and closes. She turns and examines my puzzled expression. "Who's on the phone? Why the weird look? Gramps, can you answer me?"

Placing the phone on mute, I ask, "Is this interview your idea of a joke?" Her body language reveals nothing.

"Huh?" Now her bewildered look makes me believe she is innocent. Pointing at the picture window, she spots her two other visiting cousins outside, soaking up sunrays. I need to concentrate on this call. While chatting with Angelina, I have already missed out on some facts the caller is spouting. Angelina grabs an apple and continues through the kitchen to the screened porch of the lakeside house. The dog scampers after her through the wide-open screen door.

"Close the door!" I shout after her. They go, and the door is left open.

Unmuting the phone, I begin the conversation again. I stare at the Lucchesi family photos on the porch wall and close the screen door. The photographs appear to be observing and listening intently to this call.

"You're like a living computer. The facts about Caesar and his flying days are accurate. What's that? I guess I did follow his steps in making aviation history. Nobody ever told me that, but thanks. It's a generational thing. Flying is in the blood. How did you unearth all of this information about me?"

I am not surprised by the answer. We are all reliant on the Internet. Facts and fiction about people are available online. Static on the cell phone prevents me from hearing the words distinctly, so I follow up with a question. "Huh, you also checked the local college's archives? I'm impressed."

The caller mentions another local family's name. My brain goes on alert, and a bell rings softly in my head as I hear about their involvement with regional aviation. The memory is too distant, and there is no immediate recognition.

Sonny, my six-foot-one, muscular grandson, pops his head into the house and asks me the usual. "Hey, Gramps, when are we going to eat?"

Placing my cell phone on mute again, I ask, "Are you a part of this prank phone call?" Shaking his head, Sonny snatches a bag of cookies and goes back outside. His behavior does not reveal any finite answer. The three cousins rarely spend time together, so I wonder how they planned this superior trick on me.

"I'm sorry. I've got to cut this short. I wish you the best of luck with your aviation research project."

The caller does not let me go so easily and continues talking.

"Why would you want to meet in person? Why?" I listen carefully and reply, "You don't need to give me a gift. Okay, I suppose I can work something out for later today. How will I know who you are? Where? Okay, I'll meet you there." Nodding my head in disbelief, I scribble the time and location on a paper pad and end the call. Was this a scam phone call?

It is hard to believe the caller is genuinely interested in my life as Caesar's grandson. However, the truth is that my entire career has been up in the air. More than half a century after my grandfather's death, the Lucchesi name is linked to pioneer flying in Michigan.

Why did that phone call drain so much of my energy? I check that the cousins are safe and together outside; then I move into the bedroom off the kitchen. I take off my shoes as I sit on the side of the bed. The comfortable sneakers trigger some hidden, deeply buried memory.

I don't want to think about anything, and I certainly don't want to think about my grandfather's burial. Placing my head on the pillow, I stare at the ceiling and begin to drift off as the interviewer's question repeat in my head. My mind repeats the words "Caesar" and "funeral." It is like Houdini hypnotizing someone. As I drift off to sleep, hidden memories of the funeral from 1957 surface in my subconscious mind.

Part II
September 1957

AUTHOR'S NOTES

Attention readers—you are now ascending into the story's heart with many factual incidents, people, and places. You may proceed into Part II and return to this information below or continue reading and take note of the author's use of truth and fiction.

ALERT Fact or Fiction *ALERT*

The aviation equipment, the detailed background of the Copper Country airport locations, the names of renowned aviators, and family members are genuine.

As a reminder, conversations at the Sands, in the garden, and with Norma are flights of fiction from the author's imagination. Frank, Marina, and Eino are included to enhance the storyline and are not real characters. We direct your attention to the fact that the main characters never owned a pair of Sho-Luk shoes. However, expressing emotions while dealing with the turbulence of losing a loved one is real. The entire flight crew encourages open dialogue with others regarding grief.

Now sit back, relax, and enjoy this portion of the book.

"Fact and fiction are different truths."

—Patricia MacLachlan

Chapter 2

The funeral memory comes like a jet soaring through a cloud, with plenty of thrust and lift. I remember exactly when I first learned about sadness and loss. The funeral took place on September 7, 1957.

Conversations from the past invade my dream world. As I refocus my eyes on the open grave, I hear my father's voice say, "The burial service is almost over. Stand still. You'll feel better once we get home from the cemetery."

"It hurts," I say as I shift the weight off my sore heel. My shoes are killing me. They looked cool, but the blister on my heel is not worth it.

"At thirteen, you're old enough to know how painful it is to lose your grandfather," my father sympathizes. He comforts me with a pat on the back.

"But it's my…" I protest. I frown and glare at the shoes causing the agony. As I scratch the toe of my shoe across the gravel, my pain turns to anger. I want to blame the hurt inside of me on my shoes. No luck—my heart aches. My grandfather will be buried in minutes. What does a kid my age know about death?

An airplane flies overhead, causing me to look up—how I long to be up there.

Thoughts of my grandfather rush through me. He and I had formed a bond through aviation. Since I was three years old, he had referred to me as his apprentice copilot. We felt like we had superpowers because of our freedom when flying together.

I concentrate on the sound of the plane's engine. The buzzing of the prop as the plane passes over the cemetery moves me to escape this horrible situation. I take a step away from my father and turn to leave.

My mother notices this, makes eye contact, and mouths one word to me. Then she bows her head. Her one word has lifted my spirits.

My movement surprises my father. "What are you doing, Eugene? Where do you think you're going?" His voice fades as I dart through the crowd like a hummingbird. The cemetery is crammed with family, friends, and business associates. To create my escape route, I courageously force them to step aside. My sore feet feel less painful.

I hear the airplane fly above me again, an upscale 1956 Cessna. The three-wheel tricycle landing gear confirms its identity. I have seen pictures of it in airplane magazines.

The Cessna 172 Skyhawk came out a year ago. My grandfather and I dreamed about buying this model and joked about flying it to Italy, his homeland. He taught me the Italian word for grandfather, *Nonno*, and other Italian terms. He promised a trip to Italy with me, and I needed to be prepared.

Today, traveling to Italy is far from my thoughts, but I feel I have to be at the airstrip when the Skyhawk lands. From the flight's direction, I can tell the plane is heading to the Sands runway. The airport and the cemetery are close to each other. It is merely a matter of crossing the highway. Nonno had taken me to the Sands Airport for years, but we never drove into or visited the cemetery.

⋏　⋏　⋏

Our flying together started when I was a young tyke. We fit so well together in the cockpit. Nonno found it more challenging to get in and out of planes as we grew older. But it never stopped us. Nonno promised to help me get my pilot's license when I turned sixteen. He always kept his promises.

"Stop this behavior," a mysterious voice within my skull says, like Pinocchio's Jiminy Cricket. "Your Nonno is nowhere to be found. He's buried at a cemetery."

I refuse to listen to this Jiminy Cricket-like voice and keep moving. Nonno and I had made plans and promises. He was more than a grandfather to me; he was a flying companion, teacher, friend, and advisor. The agreement did not include his death.

My brain and body work together like a well-oiled machine. The heavy feeling of sadness and confusion leave. Now excitement and adrenaline flow. I control my world.

The wooded hillside provides the shortest distance to the airstrip as I run. The thorns of the raspberry bushes scratch and tear at my skin. My Sunday best suit becomes soiled. And my shoes no longer have the military spit shine.

I hear the disapproving voice of my inner conscience once more. "Trouble, trouble, trouble."

"Shut up, shut up," I reply, and I sprint to the rhythm of my voice.

My decision to disappear from the cemetery gives me happiness and power. My parents understand, especially my mother. Today, she read my mind, and I read her lips. I knew what she wanted me to do.

At the bottom of the hill, I see the cars whiz by me on the busy highway.

"Stop, look, listen, and think before crossing the street," the chirping inner voice reminds me. This time I listen to it. I come to a halt and gasp for air.

I notice Michigan Tech College on the left, but no cars are approaching from that way. Looking in the opposite direction, I see a single red truck, and I wait for it to pass. The timeworn airstrip is across the road. Its compacted stamp sand runway dominates the Portage Lake Waterway outside of Houghton.

I search for the Isle Royale Sands Airport entry road on the opposite side of U.S. Highway 41. My slim body compacted, I swing my arms, leaping across the roadside drainage ditch and dash across the now deserted highway.

There it is, the dirt road leading to the airfield built back in 1923. The hangars are on the far side by the water, with the runway's location closer to the main road. Even though the area has two newer airports, this aging airport is still in service.

The Cessna 172 Skyhawk flies overhead.

The familiar sound of any plane fills me with pure happiness. Nonno had wanted to own a Skyhawk, and this plane went on our wish list. He had owned at least half-a-dozen aircraft in his lifetime. I grew up letting engine sounds lull me to sleep on flights. And the purr of the prop would wake me.

The sound of the Cessna Skyhawk changes as it approaches for a landing. It brings me back to the present. I skip down the road toward the runway and mentally list Nonno's pre-landing procedures. I picture us together in the cockpit.

He would ask, "Seatbelts on?"

"Yes, check," I would say.

"Fuel selector and mixture setting? Runway visible?"

"Yes, check."

"Flaps."

"Yes, check."

"Landing lights on?"

"Yes, check."

With the runway in sight, he would always speak to himself. "Reduce throttle. Keep it low and slow."

He told me landings were one of the most dangerous times when flying a plane. He would check for carburetor ice to clear the engine. A pilot would never know if they needed the motor to power up quickly.

"Hold it; hold it." He loved saying it out loud. I would hold my breath at this crucial moment in our landings.

Nonno always had smooth landings with me. A pioneering aviator with decades of experience, he knew how to land the first time without go-arounds for a second try. Nonno's landing habits were always consistent.

"Brains before brakes," he would say. "Don't touch them. It'll get you in trouble. Gently roll on in. Don't ride the brakes. Save the brakes. Let the plane roll out and back taxi."

Nonno had told me believing you are lucky makes you lucky. Pilots were worried that reckless flying would result in accidents or crashes. The Lucchesi family loved to talk about crosswinds and close calls. Nonno's theory was that any landing you could walk away from was good. If you could reuse the plane, it was a great one.

I walk to the edge of the runway. The Cessna's final approach looks proper, the touchdown flawless. It performs a perfect landing on the stamp sand runway.

Grains of fine stamp sand sting my face. I place one hand over my eyes to protect them from sand pieces and raise my opposite arm.

I wave to get the pilot's attention. The copilot is seated next to the pilot. They were well-advised to concentrate on the landing rollout procedure. A pilot has to be mindful of his surroundings on the plane.

They ignore the skinny kid on the runway's edge. Why should they care about me? I have never met this pilot or his copilot before.

My arm drops, and my hand covers my mouth. The muscles in my stomach contract. My legs buckle, and I plop to my knees. My heart doesn't want to believe what my head knows as the truth. The emotional turbulence of grief sucks my breath out of me. The weight of reality makes my head droop. Nonno will never fly again.

"It's true, true," says that inner voice. I hate to hear it and, worse, to believe it.

Another voice enters my consciousness. This growling unfriendly sound comes from the direction of the hangars. A man shouts, "Hey, kid, what do you think you're doing? Get off the runway?"

The man runs toward me like a gorilla, ready to attack. His arms flap and try to shoo me away. I didn't notice him as the plane landed. However, he observed me the whole time. I note the visor hat with a star in one of his hands. Once he crosses the runway, he slows to a walk. His dirty working coveralls are worn and patched. He places his hat on his cropped gray hair. The wrinkled eyebrows and turned-down lips are further indications of his mood.

The sleeve of my suit jacket acts as a handkerchief. I wipe my nose and stand waiting. Whatever this mean man might say to me can't be as bad as the fact I have just absorbed. With the understanding of the reality, my shoulders slump.

Chapter 3

My feet feel dog-tired, and my legs tremble. I stand stock-still with my head bent in defeat and wait. I want to flee and turn to go.

The man pauses and catches his breath. "Stop. Don't move. Don't even think of running away. Hey, kid, I'm talking to you." He roughly grabs my shoulder and turns me toward him. His eyes check me out from top to bottom. He studies my scratched, filthy, and tear-stained face.

"Hey, look at me when I'm talking to you." We stare at each other. A look of recognition appears in his eyes. "I've seen you before."

My mind whirls in an attempt to recognize his unknown face. Nothing comes up, and I continue to inspect him.

"Hey, I know you're Caesar's grandson. You've gotten older and taller. I bet you're in high school already. Busy with basketball and the girls, huh," he says.

"No, sir, I'm thirteen." Nonno taught me to be respectful to everyone. The man's question about girls seems like a joke, but it hits me as impolite. School activities keep me busy, but not with girls.

He drops his arm, steps back, and examines me. His expression changes again, as though a light bulb has gone off in his head. My suit and the tears all add up to one thing for him.

"Hey, kid, I'd ask how Mr. Lucchesi is, but I read he died. Hey, Caesar and Geno were here a week ago. Give my condolences to the family."

Everyone in the Copper Country knows my Nonno has died. It is major news for the area. The newspaper wrote an article about him. This man's sympathetic words are like salve on a wound. The man meant well, and he knew our family.

"Thank you," I reply.

"Yup, your Grandfather Caesar's life is one for the books. He's one of the Copper Country's pioneering aviators. He taught his boys to fly if they wanted to learn, right? Your uncles Leo and Geno loved flying, but the other two, Bruno and Fred, stayed on the ground. I know the sisters, Ann and Norma, both are nice women. Swell lady, Mrs. Lucchesi; she raised a nice family. You taking good care of your grandmother during her sad days?"

"Yes, sir."

He has known our family for a long time and has watched them grow up. The tone of his voice becomes softer and kinder. My eyes raise to meet his, and a hint of a smile appears on both our faces. He smiles broadly, showing his coffee-stained teeth. He places his arm lightly on my back and nudges me to move.

"Yup, Mr. Lucchesi recognized my natural skills as a mechanic. He gave me a job here a long time ago. I never left. Your grandfather spotted my genuine interest and talent as a mechanic. He gave me a chance to work and encouraged me to learn. I wasn't much older than you back then."

"My Nonno says you gotta give everyone a chance, sometimes even a second chance."

"Come on; let's get off the runway. Never know when another plane will land."

With a sniffle and quick nose swipe on my sleeve, we move toward the remote offices by the road. The nice man takes out his handkerchief to hand it to me. He scrutinizes it and returns the grease-stained cloth into his pocket. A kind gesture, but I wipe my nose again on the sleeve.

I examine the mechanic who has spoken so highly of the Lucchesi family. His wrinkles, gray hair, and weathered face tell me his life couldn't always have been indoors.

"Hey kid, it's complicated for you to lose your grandfather. Want to talk about it?"

We continue to walk in silence. This stranger's question surprises me. No one has spent a second to ask me how I feel since Nonno died. However, I have no intention of discussing it just now.

"No, sir," I say. We keep silent. But I begin to replay the previous day's events in my mind.

Three days ago, my grandparents were a happy couple. Nonno was frail and not healthy, but both grandparents were alive and active. *Nonnie* (Italian for grandmother) took good care of us.

The weather was beautiful earlier in the week, and Nonno wanted to go for a drive with Nonnie. They drove around the Copper Country and stopped to visit and check on his service stations. When they returned home, he complained about being cold. Nonnie used the blanket from his car and wrapped it around his shoulders. She started dinner as usual. Nonno said he was tired and went to their bedroom. Dinner time came, and he never ate. I helped clean the kitchen, completed my homework, and headed to my bedroom for the night.

I lived with my grandparents so I could help them. Nonno called me his young legs. My parents could open the window and call across the garden for me since we lived so close. They kept busy with three more kids—my two younger sisters and a baby brother. I enjoyed privacy, space, and attention living with my grandparents. It worked out for everyone.

The last night Nonno was alive, I brushed my teeth, kissed him and Nonnie good night, and went to sleep. I had no idea my dream would turn into a nightmare. My life changed three days ago, and it still doesn't feel real.

"It's real, very real," my brain's nagging inner voice says again.

I shake my head to clear my mind of the past days. I am not in bed, it is daylight, and I am standing next to a stranger on the Sands airfield.

"Hey, kid, you sure you don't want to talk about something?" he asks.

"Well, I remember the last time I saw my Nonno alive. He died early Thursday morning. Uncle Geno and others were there," I say.

"You're fortunate to have known your grandfather. A mining accident got my gramps. He died underground and alone. I never knew him. Pop passed years ago, and I still miss him. They're both buried in the same cemetery as your Nonno. It's kind of like they are neighbors."

Our heads turn to search the wooded hillside across the main road for the cemetery. I do not like thinking about buried, dead people, but this guy talks about departed folks like they are still alive. And he does it in a comfortable way and with love.

"I take the family there and visit. We live in a house close to the cemetery." He points toward the green hillside. "You ran by my house, coming through the woods. Oh, I've got a daughter around your age and a son going to college. You'll understand more when you're my age."

The idea of living by a cemetery sounds spooky. I never want to be reminded of Nonno in a coffin or imagine him resting in peace. I feel an uncontrollable shiver as I imagine the winter snow heaped above the earth and Nonno in his white silk-lined coffin below the ground.

"Told you I got kids of my own now. I tell them what Pop told me, 'You live until the day you die. It's the way of life.' Everyone grieves in their manner. It's better to remember the positive things and smile. Yes, it's far better than dwelling on the negative and crying."

Remember their kindness and smile. I agree with what the mechanic says. For the first time in three days, a warm fuzzy blanket wraps itself around my heart. A hint of a genuine smile comes to my lips.

"Mr. Lucchesi had wonderful times in the golden age of aviation. Ain't quite the same now with air transportation. I worked on Wacos, Cubs, Stinsons, Ford Tri-Motors, and seaplanes. Mr. Lucchesi was a real aviator, not a pilot."

"Is there a difference?" I ask.

This question stops him in his tracks. He pushes his shoulders broader and straightens his back. He begins to talk about the differences. I would bet he loves this subject.

"An aviator is born. I can tell the difference. The type of equipment doesn't matter. An aviator takes his time to learn all about her. He's sweet and respects her." He pauses, chuckles aloud, and says, "You know I'm talking about a plane, right?"

"Yes, sir." I'm so glad he stopped to clear up the misunderstanding.

"It's a magical bond between the two that no one can explain. You feel it, or you don't. It's a partnership like a marriage. You gotta work together."

Marriage and partnerships mean little to me, but I think he has complimented my Nonno. I ask, "How is a pilot different from being an aviator?"

"Pilots are made, not born. A pilot can get all the technical stuff correct, fly a plane, and manipulate the controls at the proper time. This type of pilot views the equipment as an expensive pile of bolts, nuts, and gauges. An aviator touches it with affection. Mr. Lucchesi worked like that with a plane."

Something inside me stirs, and I know what he means. I see the connection with Nonno and his planes.

"Ah, why do I tell you this stuff? You're a kid. Maybe you'll understand if you follow your grandfather's flight plan in life." He places both his hands on my shoulders and stops. "Do you fancy you'll want to be an aviator when you grow up, kid?"

"Huh?" I leave his question unanswered and shrug my shoulders.

He points to the sky. "Hey, kid, maybe you'll be flying to the moon and beyond instead of around the world. Mr. Lucchesi believed it would happen. He hated to believe the Soviet Union would win the Space Race." The mechanic laughs and adds, "Maybe you'll be the Copper Country's Buck Rogers."

I raise my eyebrows, perplexed. The honk of a horn brings our gaze back to earth. A dusty cloud appears as a car heads in our direction.

"Is that the cavalry coming to your rescue?" the mechanic asks.

Chapter 4

The mechanic removes his cap once again. He uses it to signal to a fast vehicle approaching us. The red Texaco Star on his cap brings back memories of Nonno, his Texaco gas stations, and his fascination for new cars.

"You gotta love a fine running motor," Nonno had once told me as he closed the hood of his cutting-edge modern car. During his lifetime, he had seen significant changes in transportation.

Nonno had owned horses at one time, but he never bonded with them. Nonno thought of them as engines that pulled a wagon. What he loved was the horsepower in a mechanical machine. He owned plenty of cars, buses, and trucks. Their motors needed fuel, so he figured an excellent business would be selling gasoline. One gas pump grew into a whole lot of gas stations. He was right—gasoline was the future.

I knew little about his Texaco stations. When adults talked about business, kids did not pay attention. The grownups handled the gas business while we kids ate and played. The Lucchesi family pumped gas, sold it, and distributed it throughout the area for decades. All service station attendants' uniforms proudly wore the Texaco star.

Nonno's company now included selling aviation fuel since planes have to use it. He reasoned that flying planes would benefit the enterprise. The proudly painted logos of his particular company, Range Oil & Gas, made it easy to identify his aircraft.

The star on the mechanic's hat is unique—it is a Texaco star. He must have gotten the hat years ago from Nonno. Seeing the star makes the mechanic seem like family now, and his frank talk has made me feel better. I'm glad I left the mourners at the cemetery and came to the Sands.

Shading his eyes, I observe him examine me head to toe as the car approaches us. "Hey kid, I guess someone missed you. You ran from Forest Hill Cemetery to the Sands, right? Am I dead on?" He turns to watch the car race toward us, kicking up gravel.

I refuse to answer the mechanic's question and lower my gaze to examine my shoes. My feet begin to ache again.

He returns his gaze to study me, then slants his head, nods, and concludes, "Sunday-best clothes, showy shoes." He stops for a second and shakes his head. "Tsk, tsk, your outfit doesn't look so pressed and clean now. Look at your shoes. I reckon you ran through the bushes following the plane, and I bet you didn't wait for permission to leave."

He would win a part of that bet. However, I can still picture looking at my mother. She knew and understood me. I had her approval.

"My mother told me," I begin and stop.

He turns his back to the approaching car and studies me. "Hey, kid, I'm sorry about Mr. Lucchesi, but you've got lots to smile about when you remember him. He's one gentleman I respected and admired. He lived in the present but thought about the future. He dared to be different and always wanted to see progress." The mechanic turns around to face the car and wave a greeting. "Here comes Geno. He's your uncle, correct? Watch out, kid; he ain't smiling."

The vehicle slams to a stop in front of us. The sudden braking kicks up the fine dust and gravel. I know the driver. Uncle Geno, who is known for his friendliness, is upset. I brace myself for what will follow. He jumps out of the car and bounds toward us.

"Eugene, what the Sam Hill are you doing?" He pauses and catches his breath. The dust settles to the ground as he inspects me. "Look at you. Look at your shoes. You begged to have the shoes, and they were expensive, too. You're all messed up." He switches from a scowl to an embarrassed smile when facing the mechanic. "Thanks, Frank."

With barely a whisper, I say, "Thank you, Frank."

Pointing to me, Uncle Geno continues, "This spoiled kid ran off from the graveside service up the hill. He chased the plane like a crazed dog would chase a car." Pausing for a breath, he changes his tone and adds, "I watched the plane approach downwind, too. A sleek Skyhawk? Are the owners local?"

Before Frank can answer, Uncle Geno says, "Never mind. I'll be around here now that all this funeral stuff is over. I got to take my plane and get to the modern Houghton Memorial Airport. Teaching flight classes there next week."

Uncle Geno and Frank act as though they have known each other for a long time. I relax. However, it doesn't last long.

Uncle Geno's face gets red as he speaks again. "Stupid for Eugene to follow the plane. Even the priest noticed the commotion he made at the burial. Everyone noticed as he plowed through the crowd. The plane disrupted the service, too."

Frank comes to my defense. "Give the kid a break. Aviation is in the blood, and he's going to love flying. The kid's like his grandfather."

"Like Caesar, never," Geno says. "But Pa liked the kid's company. They spent enough time together. It started with Eugene as a toddler. Pa took him around like a pet. When Pa flew to Meigs Field in Chicago for a day, Eugene went. The boy then entered school. They didn't fly together as much, and Pa didn't travel alone. But they talked about flight plans and airplanes a lot." Uncle Geno lowers his head and whispers, "Frank, those dreams are over now."

"Come on, Geno; your Pa's death is hard on you. Mr. Lucchesi lived a full life. He was such a gentleman and a leader in aviation. You have to be so proud of all his accomplishments. We will all miss him." Frank winks at me and adds, "Eugene did appear to be Italian, with black hair and brown eyes. Geno, I thought you could be related to him."

"Thanks for handling him. Any damages from this scarecrow? Cause you any trouble?" Uncle Geno asks.

Frank and I lock eyes. "No troubles here."

Uncle Geno walks around the car to get in. He gestures for me to get in on the passenger side. "Got your dog here, Frank? How's he doing after the run-in with the skunk a week ago? Guess I'd smell him if he were here."

"Naw, he's home resting for rabbit hunting later this month. He's gonna be fine." Frank places a hand on my shoulder. "Come and see me again. We can talk about aviators and planes. You can meet Buddy the Beagle, my dog. Now let's see a smile on your face, Eugene."

"Thanks for being here, Frank. I'm glad I met you," I reply.

Frank removes his hand and walks around to the driver's side to talk as I get in on my side. "Geno, I've known your Pa for a long time. I remember the day when he flew in his red-hot Waco biplane. It made top news back in the thirties. The Lucchesi family got lots of history here." Frank and Geno nod as they each scan the dated airstrip.

The waterside hangars on Portage Lake need improvements. The Isle Royale Sands airport has served its purpose as a landing field for decades. Ben Wenberg, Caesar's flying buddy, had the brilliant idea of compacting the toxic mining mill tailings known as stamp stand to create a landing strip.

Wenberg and Lucchesi developed it in the 1920s. And everything still worked just fine when the expensive plane arrived today, well over thirty years later.

"Everything changes—planes and people. Not so busy here with the two additional airports in the area now," Frank says.

He is referring to the out-of-date Laurium Airport, established in the 1930s, and the new airport, Houghton County Memorial, which has regular commercial passenger service. The Lucchesi planes are in hangars everywhere. However, the Sands is the closest to South Range, our airport of choice.

Uncle Geno interrupts. "I'm sorry. I got to get to Ma's house, Frank. Thanks again for keeping an eye on the kid. Tell me, what size shoes do you wear? Need a spotless pair?"

Frank either does not hear him or chooses not to reply.

As Geno turns over the ignition in his 1956 Jeep utility wagon, he starts rolling up the window. Frank puts his hand on the glass and stops him.

"Tell Mrs. Lucchesi and the family I will never forget him. I'm going to smile thinking about all those early days together with Caesar at the Sands. The wife says—"

"Yah, yah," Geno interrupts. "I got to get going. I'm sorry, Frank."

"And Eugene," Frank says as he leans into the window close to Geno, "maybe you'll grow up to be a pilot someday." Frank steps back and puts both his hands by his side.

Geno rolls up his window and starts the engine. He burns rubber as the car speeds from the scene. Frank disappears in a cloud of dust. As we drive away, I wonder whether anybody in Italy ever asked Caesar, when he was thirteen, if he had aviation in his blood.

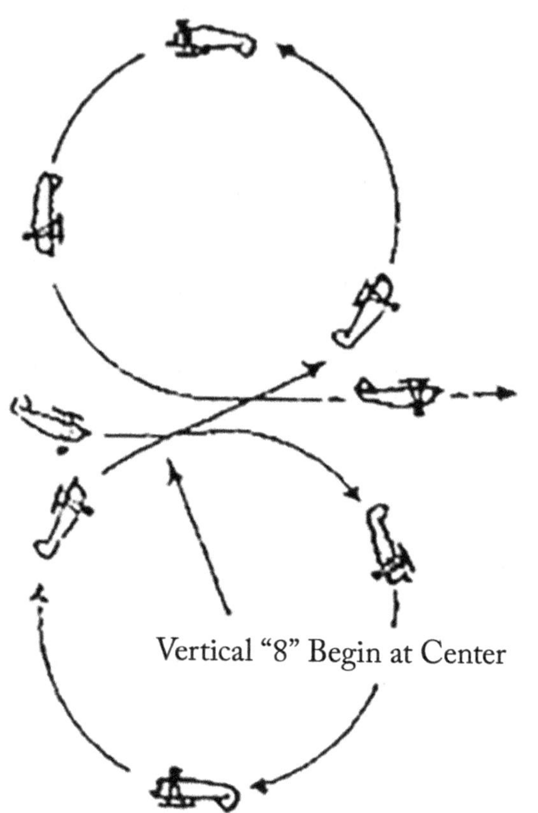

Vertical "8" Begin at Center

Chapter 5

We turn right onto U.S. Highway 41, leaving the dirt airport road in the rearview mirror. "Is everyone gone from the cemetery?" I ask Uncle Geno.

He never answers.

"Are we going back there or to South Range?" Continued silence fills the car.

Uncle Geno is focused on the road, so I am not sure he heard me. I do not want to ask again. We drive past the driveway that leads uphill to the cemetery. It answers my question—the next stop will be South Range. We continue driving, and I remember overhearing a conversation a few months earlier about why Nonnie chose the family plot in Houghton rather than the South Range cemetery.

It seems like Nonnie always wanted to move to a city. She loved to shop, and South Range had its limitations. On the other hand, Caesar loved the small village, and he had no interest in moving. She would laugh and tell people her wish would eventually come true; they would sleep forever in a city. And it was for this reason that she bought the cemetery plot in the City of Houghton.

I sink even lower in my seat as I reflect on the days since Nonno's death on Thursday.

My daily routines had been unusual yet exciting. The days flew by with all the activities and planning in the house, and no one made me go to school on Friday. Instead, I visited with families and played with cousins my age. Nonno's death seemed unreal. The cousins never sat around and discussed sad stuff.

Our local priest came to the house and made service arrangements. Neighbors brought us food—the treats I liked best of all.

"Sorry to hear about your grandfather's passing. Here—enjoy my ravioli," an Italian neighbor said. Another Finnish neighbor said, "Let the grownups worry about things besides cooking. Enjoy my nisu bread."

Someone at the house kindly accepted the food. My cousins and I gorged ourselves like bears out of hibernation.

Nonnie did not cook at all. She did not smile much either since Nonno had died. People around her tried to make things problem-free. Nonnie let them.

"Ma, I'll handle the church choir music."

"Don't worry about the gravestone. It's done."

"Ma, what's there to eat?"

The kitchen remained the heart of Nonnie's home. We hosted strangers at the Lucchesi kitchen table and fed them all the time. Nonnie handled it with skill and grace. She had married Nonno over fifty years ago, and they had operated well together.

Other adults called Nonnie "Jennie." I had also heard Nonno whisper in Italian, "*Mia dolce Gelsomina.*" I would have to remember to call her sweet Gelsomina when she felt blue.

All of Nonno and Nonnie's kids spoke Italian. Nonno had wanted to learn English. He had always asked me about my schoolwork, and we had studied together over the years. Things would be different now.

A noise startles me. Uncle Geno is clearing his throat. Out of the corner of my eye, I look at his profile. He reminds me of Roman emperors. His movie-star looks could have made him rich in Hollywood, but he chose and loved flying like Nonno. I wonder what his life might have been like if he had left isolated northern Michigan. He has never ventured away from home or family. His pa decided everything, and Nonno's nickname was "The Boss."

"What was it like to have Nonno as a father?" I ask Uncle Geno. I sit straighter in the seat. He must have heard me because he repeats the words under his breath. For the second time today, my lip-reading talents come in handy.

"Pa knows," he starts to say. I watch his Adam's apple bob up and down before he corrects the word to its past tense. "Pa knew— he knew how to keep himself and others busy. We all worked for him. I don't know where or what I'd be without him as The Boss. He treated his grandkids better than his kids. How do you think it would feel if you were his son, Eugene?"

My face flushes, and I stammer out my reply. "I reckon it'd be tough."

Uncle Geno exhales loudly and nods. "The Boss wanted the latest in technology. Cars, buses, trucks, planes—if it had a motor, he loved it. Pa would have had gasoline to drink instead of goat's milk."

We both crack up over that one. However, I know Nonno could have digested goat's milk easier. The mood inside the car lightens. I curl my toes up and down to get the blood circulating again.

"Didn't you feel proud of Nonno last year when he got his college degree?"

Raising the corner of his upper lip slightly, Uncle Geno lashes out his response. "It took Leo and Bruno some years to get their college degrees. They were in their forties. And Nonno only got an honorary alumni certificate. It wasn't a degree. College isn't for everyone."

I had done it again. The special day at the college in 1956 brought bad memories for Uncle Geno. He had achieved so much in his lifetime. What irritated him about his brother and father receiving those degrees? Uncle Geno's hateful statements might be his method of expressing his sadness. He should be able to deal with grief better than kids.

We arrive in Houghton's bustling downtown and drive by the East Houghton Texaco filling station. It has a crackerjack location in town and is a moneymaker for the company. A massive sign in the window reads Closed—Family Funeral.

Uncle Geno glances over and reads the sign. "Humph! There is no money coming in today from there."

As we continue into the city, my eyes close, and my sense of smell arouses a delicious memory. I picture a crisp puff pastry's golden shell filled with cold, creamy vanilla-flavored custard. I remember when Nonno and I stopped at the Crown Bakery for his treat, cream puffs. I lick my lips. When the tires strike a pothole, I bite my tongue accidentally.

"Oh, fudge," I say.

Uncle Geno's words startle me. "No, I'm not stopping at the bakery for fudge."

"Nonno loved their cream puffs. We could...." My voice trails off into silence.

Uncle Geno grunts and continues to drive. We both stare straight ahead as though we wear horse blinders.

My left foot starts to ache. I bend over to loosen my shoe and flip the closure open. After I pull my foot out, I notice dried blood on the heel of my sock. The pain does not bother me as much as Uncle Geno's weird behavior.

"Let's listen to the radio," I suggest.

A famous advertising jingle plays on the radio. Uncle Geno gawks at my ruined new-fangled shoes instead of the road, and I sing along and click my fingers to the jingle.

Uncle Geno snaps off the radio. "No catchy jingles. Be quiet." He takes one hand off the steering wheel and uses his fingers to rub the side of his forehead.

The jingle runs through my mind as we drive on. It reminds me of the day I went shopping for shoes with Nonno. I close my eyes, rub my knees, and remember every detail from that afternoon.

I can hear Nonno's voice with its Italian accent as he told me we needed fashionable dress shoes. "Friends and shoes—choose both wisely," he told me.

"*Adiamo*," he said.

I repeated, "Let's go," first in English and then Italian, "Adiamo, Nonno."

We talked about school, basketball, and even girls as we drove. The radio played the commercial shoe jingle. He laughed, and we sang it together.

Once in the shoe department, I persuaded him to buy us a pair. The shoes were the most recent 1957 version and the latest look afoot. The shoes would be comfortable and straightforward for Nonno to put on and take off with their adjustable closure.

I pitched the shoes as sharp, handsome-looking, and long-lasting. It would be a wise investment, and Nonno deserved them. I also found the perfect pair for a modern thirteen-year-old boy on the go like me. Nonno bought the adult version, and I got the matching kid-size shoes. At our show-and-tell over dinner, Nonnie scolded us both for being tricked by the creative commercial. As Nonno and I sang the ingenious tune, we laughed over the matching Shu-Loks.

Shaking my head to come back to the present, I focus on my aching foot. Somehow, I do not object to my Shu-Loks after remembering the memorable shopping trip with Nonno.

Chapter 6

We continue the ride in silence toward South Range. I twist my head to see the best view of Houghton and Hancock, the twin cities. The Portage Lake bridge links the two towns and connects the extreme tip of northern Michigan to the rest of the state. A modern bridge will soon replace the run-down iron truss double-decker one. Everyone in both cities is excited about it.

"Have you heard anything about the elevator-type bridge?" I ask. Uncle Geno remains silent, so I focus on the scenery. My eyes drift toward the top of Quincy Hill.

The historic Number 2 Quincy Mineshaft-Rockhouse remains a well-known landmark at the top of the steep hill on the Hancock side. We all know Nonno once worked underground mining for copper at the Quincy Mine. He had shared stories of the dangers and horrors of working in the damp, dark underground. He left the job to deliver goods in a horse-drawn wagon between mines on the surface. Nonno used to joke about never descending into the ground until it was six feet deep. I gulped. Now he was finally achieving his wish. The car surges forward as we reach the top of Van Orden's Hill.

"I will stop at the Atlantic Mine gas station and call Ma and tell everyone I got you," Uncle Geno says. "They all should be there."

After this long morning, I have two things on my mind—food and family. My folks will understand my absence, and they will not freak out.

"Your parents are mad as heck with you for running away and making us all worry."

"I'm sorry, but I thought my mother—"

Uncle Geno curls his top lip to his nose as though he whiffs a skunk's scent. "Knock it off. Save that stuff for your mother."

"But my mother—"

"You lost it today. Your mother, my sweeeeet sister Norma, wants to box your ears for not listening to her at the cemetery."

"But she told me—"

"She told you? She told you to interrupt the service and make everyone worry about you? Make me waste my time fetching you?"

"But I thought—"

"No, you didn't think. You didn't stop to think of others."

"The plane, and Nonno, and…." I stopped speaking.

"She figured out why you went to the Sands. You know she spent time with Pa there as a kid. He flew Norma to many places, and she did her solo flight out of there at sweet sixteen. Pa called her his '*dolce pilot*' and look at her now. She may have Lucchesi flying blood in her veins, but she's married, with four kids, and grounded. Yes, I'd say pretty well-grounded." He snickers at his unkind joke.

With my lips sealed tightly, I visualize my mother spelling out the two-letter word at the cemetery. A trickle of doubt enters my mind. Had I seen what I wanted to see?

The twenty-foot sign pole with the Texaco red star looms ahead for the Atlantic Mine station. The dairy truck pulls out, and we drive into the empty spot by the Sky Chief gas pump. The two uniformed service attendants recognize the Jeep and come over to welcome Uncle Geno.

They greet us with words of condolence as Uncle Geno rolls down his window. One worker moves closer to Geno to share a story. Nobody notices me as I listen to their conversation.

"If your father had not extended credit back in the Depression, we'd have lost the farm. That's over twenty years ago, but it's not forgotten. Sorry, we couldn't make the funeral, but you know how it goes with the station open."

The shorter attendant finishes washing our windshield. "Mr.

and Mrs. L stopped here Wednesday. We performed the full service on their car and topped off the gas tank. 'Put it on my account,' he said and tipped as he usually did. I've saved that special quarter he gave me. Such a great man."

The two attendants bob their heads and listen to Geno describe Nonno's last moments. I wish I could close my eyes and not hear what he says.

"He wanted me there at his bedside. Picture it. He's in bed, still wearing clothes from the car ride. Believe it or not, nobody even removed his shoes. I removed them. Say, what's your shoe size?"

"His new shoes?" I blurt out. Uncle Geno doesn't answer my question, and the attendants remain focused on his tale. They devour the gossip like starved seagulls.

"Then, without a word, Pa reached into his pocket and handed me the ring of keys to all the stations." Uncle Geno pauses and waits for their surprising response.

"Wow! It makes you The Boss now."

"Correct."

The two employees simultaneously take mini-steps back from the car and glance at each other.

Getting out of the vehicle, Uncle Geno says, "I need to use the phone."

"It's all yours, Boss. No sweat."

One attendant sprays, wipes, and cleans the remaining windows on the Jeep. The second checks the air pressure in the tires. They chat as they work. When they move to my side of the car, I overhear their comment.

"Geno has a tough act to follow."

I slump farther in the car seat and begin to recite the twelves multiplication table. It shifts my attention away from Uncle Geno's blathering.

I close my eyes and create a chalkboard with a double-digit problem. Scratching my head, I try to recall the simplest way to solve the problem. What was the answer to twelve times fourteen? They dubbed me a whiz child in elementary school, but the numbers are not whizzing through my mind today. My brain goes blank. I grind to a standstill and wait for Uncle Geno.

He returns to the vehicle, opens the door, and slithers back into his seat like a snake. We leave the station without a wave, and he never tipped the attendants. Nonno always left a tip.

Questions about the gas station business pop into my mind. I peek at Uncle Geno and know today's behavior will not last forever. He seems tired, sad, and mad. This Geno is not the Uncle Geno the family remembers and adores. Nonno had put his faith in him to run the business.

"Congratulations, Uncle Geno. Nonno made a first-class choice by selecting you as the next Boss. Can you tell me more about the business?"

His expression changes. The muscles in his face lose their tension, and a smile appears. I even hear him exhale before he begins to speak.

"Thanks. I appreciate you saying that, Eugene. I haven't been my best the past few days. Stressed is a better word. There's plenty of history with Pa. He made things happen, and I'm going to miss him. Pa was the experienced Boss."

My arms twitch with an urge to hug him. I resist because he is driving. "Uncle Geno, you have tremendous shoes to fill now, and you'll make a swell boss, too. You've been there every step of the way."

"Thanks. You're right. You want some history, huh? I've got some facts for you, Eugene. Pa's first gas pump was in front of the South Range house in 1918. Two years later, we started the garage.

He added Range Oil & Gas Company in 1924. A year or two later, we introduced selling gas to the public. In 1932, we switched all oil companies over to one—Texaco."

"It's been Texaco all my life," I say. "Sky Chief, Sky Chief. Fire Chief. Fill up with Fire Chief." The Texaco Star Theater's television jingle flows out of my mouth like high octane gasoline.

Uncle Geno chuckles, "You know he had the bus company before the gas stations. What kept a bus moving—petrol, yes?"

I nod and add, "A bus company; that's cool."

"More like frozen. In the winter, Pa invented plows and hired men to keep the roads cleared. Snow didn't stop him, and he kept the buses on schedule. No wonder Fred went to California. He had to thaw out from driving those unheated buses all winter."

"I'm so glad Uncle Fred and Aunt Chickie got here in time from California. They're going to stay with Nonnie again," I say.

"Fred is full of stories and loves an audience. You'll get all the history you want. As a kid, Fred worked for Pa in the livery stable. Pa always knew vehicles would replace horses. He was a true pioneer in transportation. I guess he earned the honorary degree from college by working hard and not in a classroom. The Boss said preparation and opportunity made his luck. Pa's the real rags-to-riches immigrant story."

"How about Nonno's flying history? What made him get interested in planes?" I ask.

Uncle Geno's mood continues to improve with this question. If Nonno was known as the Sky King, his son Geno could be regarded as the Prince of the Sky. Uncle Geno's stories of our family history make the miles fly past.

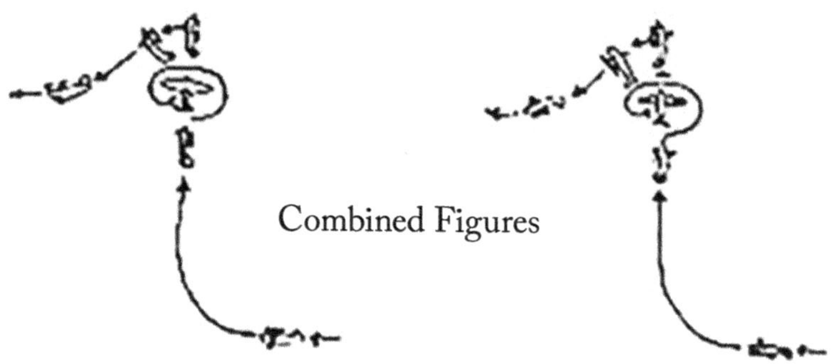

Combined Figures

Chapter 7

"Talking about the past makes me feel better than being in the present," says Uncle Geno.

"That's good. I like it, too. Please share more flying stories." I study his face, and the two deep furrows between his eyebrows disappear. Talking about planes must agree with him. He continues with the storytelling.

"Pa had two early flying buddies. They were known as the Keweenaw pioneering aviators. You heard Pa talk about Wenberg and Miller. Those three were some of the first to build, own, trade, and fly airplanes in the Copper Country sky. Ever see the printed newspaper article Ma saved about them? You were brainy enough to read it when it came out."

"I did, Uncle Geno. The newspaper photographer came to South Range and took a picture in Nonnie's kitchen of the three of them. They also used the picture of Nonno standing by his Waco F-2 on the Sands in the paper."

Uncle Geno nods his head in approval. "You ask why Pa wanted to fly?"

I lean toward him to hear every word and watch the smile on Geno's face grow. We both are in seventh heaven talking about Nonno's flying history. "Simple answer, he loved it."

"When, where, how?"

"The barnstormers, the daredevil pilots that came to the area, got him interested in flying. They'd sell people rides on their planes. Perhaps around 1917. Pa got hooked, and it was love on the first flight. He was obsessed by the early 1920s. Then he took flying lessons in Escanaba at twenty bucks an hour," says Uncle Geno.

"Well, that's not too expensive," I reply.

His loud and hearty belly laugh fills the car. Even in sorrow, the joyful sound brings relief. Uncle Geno takes his hand closest to me and ruffles my hair affectionately.

"What's so funny?" I ask. "I could save twenty dollars."

"You're the math whiz. Figure it out. In 1925, the government passed the minimum wage at sixteen cents an hour. A man was sitting pretty to make sixty-five bucks a week. It didn't go very far if you had a family to feed. You never heard that in school, did you?"

"No, sir," I reply.

"Do instructors ever teach you about the Four Continents flight in school? It happened in 1927. Ring a bell?"

I shake my head. Everyone has heard about the Wright Brothers, Lindbergh's trip, and Amelia Earhart. What did four continents have to do with Nonno and aviation?

"I'm telling you this because the aviators were all Italian. Pa made us memorize their names: Pinedo, Zacchetti, and del Prete. Pa bragged about their Savoia-Marchetti S.55 airplane named the Santa Maria. It departed in 1927 from Rome, flew to Australia, next to Asia, then over the waters to South America, and ended in North America."

I name the four continents to myself and admire those brave pioneering Italian aviators. It could not have been an easy accomplishment. I will have to look it up and read more.

"Ever see the pictures of del Prete that Ma saved from the newspaper?" he asks.

"Sure, I recognize that name. He was from Lucca, Italy, just like them. Nonno respected him and kept the 1928 Italian newspaper article about his funeral," I answer.

"Another treasured piece of paper, huh. Ma and little Bruno went to the church funeral in Lucca during their trip back in '28. She hopes someone will appreciate all the junk she is saving."

"Nonnie also showed me her treasures from the Century of Progress Exposition in Chicago, all in the same box. My mother talked about being there in 1933 when she was ten. Were you or Nonno ever there?"

"Not me, but Pa went later in July. He missed seeing Italy's Royal Air Force. Ever learn about General Italo Balbo in school?"

"Never."

"You should check the encyclopedia and study Italian aviators. You've got 100 percent Italian blood flowing through your body. Be a proud Italian-American."

"Nonnie showed me a newspaper clipping with about twenty-four hydroplanes that landed on Lake Michigan in tight formation during the exposition. Was Chicago's Balbo Street named after General Balbo?"

"She kept that article, too? Ma saved too much of that dated stuff. Who will ever look at it again? It's garbage; she should get rid of it. What is she going to do with all of Pa's things? Make a museum? Write a book?" He laughs before asking me another question. "Teachers in school ever teach you who's buried in Grant's tomb?"

The ill-mannered Uncle Geno has returned. Is this how adults grieve for loved ones? He becomes quiet, and I observe the reappearance of the frown lines. The discussion makes him feel good, and I want to ask him more questions about flying.

Uncle Geno's hands grip the steering wheel tighter. He mumbles, "Why did they call the priest instead of a doctor?"

My shocked face shows I have no answer for my frustrated uncle. I hope he can talk to another adult about his feelings. Maybe it all has to do with him being the new Boss? The closer we get to South Range, the more his agitation increases. Uncle Geno stares at the paved highway, and I turn to the side window.

As we drive past South Range's cemetery road, I remember my baby brother, buried there, who never had a chance to grow up. Nonno had lived to be eighty, but the baby, named Caesar, had died at three months. Now both Caesars are gone. Could they be united somewhere above? The thought makes me grin inside, and the tightness in my shoulders eases. Uncle Geno clears his throat to speak. "I'm going to my house before going to Ma's place. Come inside and clean yourself. You're Caesar Lucchesi's grandson. No dirty, tear-stained face for you. You're a young man, and men don't cry."

Poor Uncle Geno. I had seen a man cry—his father, my Nonno. I remembered where we were, the music playing on the radio, and the tears in his eyes. It surprised and worried me. I had asked Nonno if he was in pain.

"I'm fine. I'm feeling the feelings. The music makes me happy. You make me happier."

He told me certain emotions and feelings brought tears to his eyes. Sometimes it was better to cry than get mad. Nonno said there were tears for pain, beauty, and sadness. I even remember his precise words when he said, "You'll learn with age real men can cry."

"I appreciate you watching out for me and the ride home," I say to Uncle Geno. He abruptly twists the radio knob to signal the end of our conversation. The announcer at the radio station catches my attention.

"Listen; he's talking about Auntie Ann," I say. The announcer says he's dedicating the next song to her and the family in memory of Caesar Lucchesi.

We both recognize the artist's name. It astonishes me to hear Elvis Presley sing this song. We listen to the music without saying a word. Uncle Geno relaxes his jaw, and his face softens. Tears well, threatening to roll down his cheeks. When the song, "Peace in the Valley," ends, he turns off the radio.

"That man is the most talented singer in the world. He sings somewhere between a baritone and a tenor. His rendition touched my heart and soul. He's the best singer I know."

My jaw flies open in disbelief and amazement. Elvis is a hit with the kids, particularly the shrieking female fans. I never would have thought Uncle Geno could appreciate him.

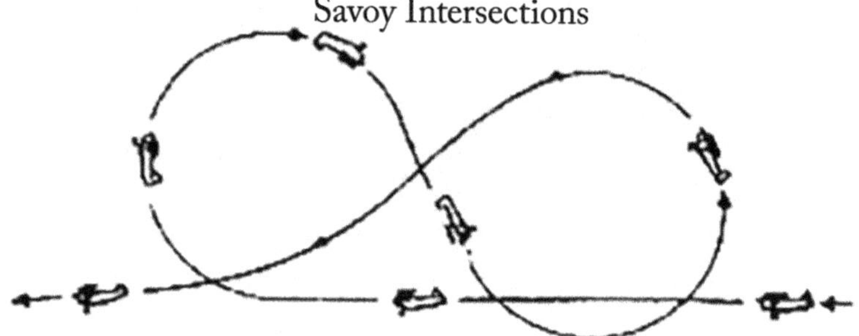
Savoy Intersections

Chapter 8

Uncle Geno's reaction to the music blows me away. Allowing his sadness to show, I hope, will give him peace. The gospel hymn about the tame wolves in a valley repeatedly plays in my mind even with the radio turned off.

"Close your mouth, or you'll catch flies." His comment embarrasses me.

As I study my shoes, I remember when Nonno and I mocked Elvis as we joked about a pair of navy suede shoes. I try to polish my scuffed shoes on my pant leg and think about his other famous song, "Blue Suede Shoes."

"Uncle Geno, you're a first-class musician. Nonno often told me how you could play any instrument by ear. He said you even composed music, and he liked it all."

"Really? Thanks. He never told me that."

Everything looks normal as we drive into South Range. Many buddies play Saturday baseball in the cow field to the left. They play and act like nothing in the world has changed their lives. They are carefree and happy. A twinge of irritation stiffens my spine. I am jealous of their happiness. Why did things have to change?

As we past Second Street, I see Whealkate Bluff, the high hill above the village on the west side of town. In school, I learned the name came from early miners exploring for gold and silver. However, the real treasure in the area happened to be pure native copper.

Copper mines needed workers. Foreigners came and worked the mines. New York City had nothing over the Copper Country as a melting pot. The Italians, Finns, Slavs, Germans, Irish, and Cornish had come to work the mines years ago. Some mines still operate today, but not like in Nonno's heyday.

We turn onto Main Street. I glance at our closed Texaco service station. As we drive by our station, I watch Uncle Geno take a hand off the steering wheel and touch something in his pocket, and I hear the clink of keys.

Uncle Geno mumbles, "Can't believe he waited so long to give up these keys."

My empty stomach makes a sound, but I have enough brains to keep my lips zipped. I begin to worry about my entrance at Nonnie's. What kind of reception awaits me?

Uncle Geno must be a mind reader because he picks up on my case of jitters. He says, "Your mother is displeased with your leaving the service. Best find her first and apologize. You can fill your belly after that."

We drive over the embedded train tracks crossing the street and continue past the Jacobsville red sandstone community hall.

The town of South Range knows how to plan elaborate Fourth of July festivities. People from all around the country travel to this famous range town to cluster around the stone structure. South Range goes all out for this celebration. Parades, fireworks, contests for young and old, with tons of folks in town. The kids fill up on candy, and the adults visit.

I doubt there will be candy today, but adults will be visiting Nonnie's. I will find food and my cousins. I tell myself, *Easy in and easy out, slippery as an eel.*

"Don't think you can slip in and out unnoticed at Nonnie's," says Uncle Geno. "You made us all worry about you. Such a selfish act. I'd call it a terrible decision, Eugene."

He decreases the speed and cruises to his house behind the community building. Uncle Geno knows his wife and daughter Janie are already at Nonnie's. After the car stops in front of the house, he expects me to accompany him inside.

When Uncle Geno unlocks the house's front door, out bounds his spotted black and white dog. "How's my baby? Yes, Daddy's home now. Did ya miss me?" The dog circles him with welcoming barks. Uncle Geno vigorously scratches behind the dog's ears and kisses him on his head.

He chatters with his dog, revealing plenty of emotion and concern for him. He has never shown any of this concern for me. Today, his behavior with me did not match his jobs as our village president, the fire chief, or my favorite relative.

He holds the front door for me, and I go in, followed by the energetic Dalmatian. I stop in the kitchen. The counter space overflows with fruit baskets, potted plants, and vases of cut flowers. Sympathy cards addressed to Geno remain sealed and piled on the table.

"Use the bathroom downstairs. Wash and then head to Nonnie's." He and the dog, Chief, scurry upstairs.

Aviation blood flows through Uncle Geno's veins. He loves to fly. The plaques, prizes, and photographs decorating the wall prove this. He is part owner and flight instructor in the Lake Superior Aviation Company. He also helps manage the Texaco Range Oil & Gas. And he has his civic responsibilities. All this keeps a fellow busy.

After washing my hands, I leave his house to walk to Nonnie's place. I study the village center with the church on one end and my grade school on the other.

Nonno told me his choices were either damnation or education. He seldom entered the church. However, he loved to learn. Nonnie donated time and money to the church. Nonno believed the mere act of being charitable was its reward. Both were cheerful givers in their ways.

"Sorry to hear about your gramps." A man's voice comes from the shadow of the abandoned train depot. Allie, a South Range general store owner, strolls into the sunshine. He is also a close family friend because he grew up with my aunt and uncles.

"It's me, Allie. I'm heading back to the market. Are you proud of yourself? You upstaged Gramps with your disappearing act at his burial. Your mother has some choice words for you. Be prepared. You know she can swear like a sailor in three different languages. Being the baby in the family, she knows how to fight. We've all seen her temper." From deep inside his belly comes some Santa-like ho, ho, ho. He continues to his store, singing a Christmas song.

His talk about fighting reminds me of something Nonnie had shown me in her attic—my mother's birthday gift from her four brothers when she turned eight. They gave her a pair of boxing gloves. My mother was known for being generous and kind but also a firecracker—fizz, hiss, bang.

What should I expect? A hug or a haymaker punch? I hate conflict. My unfilled stomach twists and turns, anticipating our meeting.

My dusty shoes take me closer and closer to Nonnie's like an automated robot. The fancy footwear propels me up the stairs and smack dab in the middle of Nonnie's kitchen. My heart races, and like a deer in the headlights, I freeze and stare into the crowded room.

Chapter 9

The kitchen table is overflowing with cheese platters, hunks of Italian bread, pasta dishes, molded Jell-O salads, and cold cuts. My eyes feast on the sight, and the immediate hunger wins. My mother can wait.

I squeeze in between adults who are chatting, arguing, and eating. My father spots me as I am stuffing my face with prune tarts. He weaves his way through the crowd to get to me. In his quiet manner, he touches my shoulder, putting me at ease.

"You gave us all a scare today. Your mom's furious because you ran away. We realized why you left and where you went. Uncle Geno volunteered to get you." He rubs my back and whispers, "Death and grief are hard to understand. We can talk about it later, but there's something you must do right now." He points to the prune tarts on my plate. "Quit eating these. Save me some. They're my favorite," he teases. Then he becomes serious again. "Talk with your mom. Then join your cousins in the garden."

He pushes me away from the prune tarts plate and directs me to the main bedroom. I move slowly through the crowd until I come to a halt at the closed door.

The bedroom is conveniently located off the kitchen, but it provides little privacy. I hear soft sobs coming from behind the closed door. I stand motionless, like a soldier at attention. No, I am not prepared for this. I march away after making a 180-degree turn.

I make my way out of the crowded kitchen, down the stairs, and outside with a full stomach. I squeeze between some of the parked cars to cross the street. At the garden gate, I freeze. Like spiders crawling on my back, a creepy feeling halts my entrance. I turn and study the apartment I just left. The Venetian blinds are down in my grandparents' bedroom. The windows face the road. Who was looking at me? It gives me the creeps.

I continue to stare at the cement block two-story building we call home. I know every inch of it. The Italian-style building has served many purposes since 1909. The ground floor was once a livery stable, and we still use it as a garage, storage room, and office.

The ground-level oversized garage has two doors, one for the entrance and one for the alley exit. Over the back door, Nonno has nailed a rusty iron horseshoe saved from his livery business. He said it would turn bad luck into good luck if you worked hard.

Nonno had installed an automatic garage door opener on the First Street garage door, making it easy to drive his long luxury car inside. He had also constructed an elevator that connected the garage to the living quarters upstairs. Nonno had to pull on the elevator cord to make it go up or down.

I loved the unique aroma of garlic from Nonnie's kitchen and the hint of gasoline from Nonno's garage. Nonno enjoyed mechanical things, but Nonnie had magical skills with food, plants, and animals. Nonnie always talked about the rolling hills of Tuscany, the sun-kissed vineyards, and hundred-year-old olive trees. She came to America in 1902 and still missed the farmland. Nonno had satisfied her need for farming with ample land for an orchard, garden, and chicken coop. She only had to cross the street to reach her heaven on earth.

Now, I stand outside the garden gate and think about her children and grandkids. We have all worked in the two lots that form her garden. Nonnie's motto is "Everyone eats, everyone works."

A girl's voice asks, "Eugene, are you waiting for a written invitation? Come on in." My cousin Janie stands inside the garden, under the lilac tree. "I guess my dad found you," she says and opens the gate for me. Heading toward the grape arbor, she adds, "We need your help picking the ripe grapes. You're tall and can reach them. Besides, Nonnie won't yell at you. Your younger sisters are over there, picking raspberries. They aren't listening to my warning words about not getting dirty or eating berries. Why can't they follow the rules?"

Janie and I are close in age. She follows the rules and worries too much. The grownups like to ask her questions because she answers them truthfully. Janie can't keep a secret. As her glasses slip down her nose, she tattles about everyone. She pushes her glasses into place with one hand and points to the grape arbor and the chaos there.

My younger cousins are acting recklessly by standing on an unstable table, and Janie has reason to be jittery. They are jumping and trying to grasp a bunch of grapes. No one thinks about the danger. The safety patrol kid in me comes out.

"Stop! I'll help you," I shout and jog over the manicured lawn bordered by neat rows of flowers. "Get off the table and let me do it." I grab a bunch of grapes with a short stretch and hand the clusters to the greedy hands below. Next, I reach higher for another bunch. I hear something rip and jump off the table. My cousins pounce on me before I am even on the ground.

"Look, he ripped his jacket."

"Auntie Norma's gonna have a cow. You've ruined your shoes."

"Oh, boy, you're in trouble. Where have you been?"

"Why did you take off from the funeral?"

They circle me and pelt me with all their questions. I remain in the center and hold my tongue. I need help to defend myself against this gang. Where is Charles? His kid sisters are here and act like terriers yipping at my heels. My two sisters are dreadful and show no mercy. I press my lips together in the hope that they will vanish.

"Shut up and go pick flowers!" comes a shout from behind a bush.

At last, Charles comes to my rescue. He springs from the bushes, snarls, and bares his teeth. The girls scatter and laugh, and the mood changes. My two sisters with raspberry-stained fingers come over and hug me. Then they fly off to join the others.

Charles takes pride in his physique. He does not represent the weakling version pictured in a Charles Atlas advertisement. Instead, he could model for Charles Atlas. Although we are the same age, we have different hobbies and body types. Best of all, we are good buddies. At age thirteen, we both are on the verge of manhood. However, nobody would dare call Charles a skinny scarecrow. I greet Charles with a sigh of relief.

He greets me with a buddy punch to the shoulder and says, "What's buzzin', cuzzin?"

Chapter 10

My numero uno, my favorite, number-one cousin, Charles, makes
me feel good again. Feelings of guilt vanish. My body feels calmer
than it has all day.

I look at Charles and ask, "What were those girls thinking?
They kept pestering me with questions. Heck, I don't understand
what I did today. All I know is I feel terrible. I can't get used to the
idea that Nonno is dead. How about you, Charles?"

"Forget those silly girls. They're too young to understand.
They'll never remember this day as we will." Charles moves closer
to me. "My mother and I had a buddy-buddy talk today about her
brother dying. It happened long ago—World War II, you know."

I don't know what this has to do with Nonno's funeral, but I
listen as Charles talks.

"My mom's brother died in Pearl Harbor, the start of the Second
World War. Talk about everything changing in a flash. Mom says
we're blessed to have a funeral for Nonno because her family never saw
her brother or even got to say goodbye. All they got was a flag."

I decide to tell Charles about my final hours with Nonno. As
I tell him about the evening, he looks at the ground. "I went into
the bedroom to say good night to him. Nonno didn't say anything
to me, but his warm hand squeezed mine. I thought I'd see him for
breakfast the following day. No one told me he was dying." I stop for
a deep breath of air. "But he died. Today when I heard the plane fly
over the cemetery, I wanted it to be Nonno. I ran there, wishing he
was the one coming in for a landing." My voice cracks, "I know the
truth. Dead is dead." I sigh.

"Yup," Charles states, "when you die, your heart stops, you
don't breathe, you don't eat. Dead is dead." He looks across the

street to the building. "Well, we're alive, breathing, but we're not eating. Want to go back upstairs and grab some cheese, salami, and bread?" He pats his abdominal muscles and angles his head, waiting for an answer.

There is one question I want to ask Charles before ending this conversation. "Today while in church—um," I stammer and stop.

Charles reads my expression and says, "Spit it out, Cuz."

"Well, what did you think about the service today?"

To emphasize his message, he uses both hands like an Italian. "We knew Nonno as a grandpa, a classic man who kept himself busy. Flat out, we loved him and all that neato stuff, but today I listened and learned."

I nod to encourage him to continue.

"It surprised me to hear how others spoke about him. I'm talking about the big shots who came to the funeral and shook hands. Listening to their praise, I realized our Nonno was a big deal. Caesar Lucchesi was a significant person in our Copper Country. We're lucky we got his blood in our veins. The funeral was a major league deal," he says. "Nonno was a big, colossal deal."

Those words ring true for me, too. At the end of the nineteenth century, Nonno came as an immigrant to America with nothing. He did better than okay. There were newspaper stories about him. I knew Nonnie would save some of the articles.

"Janie raved about the newspaper article today," Charles says. "Her mom told her it is called a eulogy when someone says so many remarkable things about a person at their funeral. His printed eulogy seemed extra special."

Charles fishes for something in the back pocket of his dressy pleated slacks. He comes up with a neatly folded newspaper clipping. With a flourish of his hand, he unfolds it and hands it to me, saying, "I can't read all the fifty-cent words printed here, but I'm going to save it forever. All the neighbors in Hancock gave us their copies. Even Betty got a copy, and she is too young to read. Have you read it, Cuz?"

"No," I say as I reach for it. The written words are extremely powerful. Charles remains motionless as I read some of it aloud.

"Self-made man, he enjoyed life." I hesitate and ask Charles if he knows what a jovial disposition means. He sighs and shrugs his shoulders. I continue to read and scan the paper.

"I like the part here about love. Listen, 'love is the most important bread and butter of life.' Nice, huh? But I don't understand how being born in humble circumstances is valuable. What does it mean?"

"You work harder if you're poor in the beginning," Charles replies.

I read a portion of the last paragraph aloud. "…both generous and proud and was well aware that generosity is giving more than you can, and pride is taking less than you need, and this was the code by which Caesar lived."

The wind dies away as I refold the *Daily Mining Gazette* editor's eulogy clipping and hand it back to Charles. Everything remains motionless in the garden. Charles finally slides it back into his pocket.

"We can never live up to that," I say.

"Nope, you're not Caesar. Gotta do your own thing. Be yourself, and be cool."

"I did my own thing this morning," I say, "and I bet I'll have a cooling-off period."

Charles laughs.

I stare at my ruined shoes. "What's the saying about walking a mile in someone else's shoes? Do you want to place another bet on whether my mother will fit into these?"

We both laugh as I point to the once new shoes.

Loops

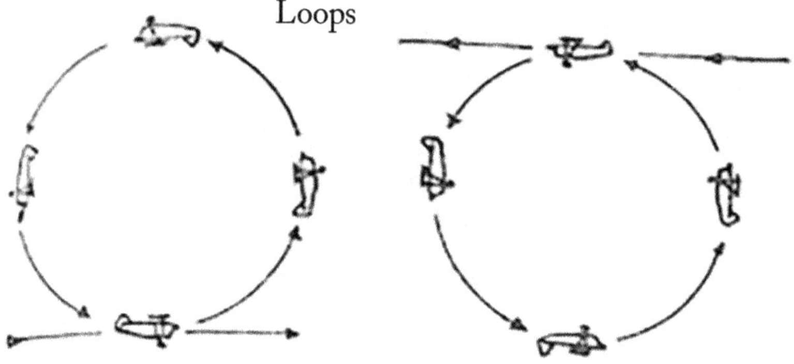

Chapter 11

Our younger cousins come begging for more grapes like a flock of clucking hens. Charles repeats his earlier performance with the girls and gets the same results.

"Grrrrr." They run, leaving us alone in the garden. Then Charles turns to me and asks, "What will you miss about our historic, venerable man? I'm talking about Nonno," he adds.

"Cream puffs. Crown Bakery's cream puffs. How about you?"

"Rides in his luxury tank. You know, his Chrysler Imperial sedan. Love it. The pushbutton windows, the automatic transmission, that V-8 engine—riding in there was a big deal."

I remind Charles about the unique sound of the car horn. "Did you ever press the horn ring? Didn't you love scaring people? They thought a boat was coming. You felt like Captain Lucchesi and crew floating over the road."

Charles continues with more personal memories. "Nonno would come to the Hancock station and ask me to clean and polish the chrome. I loved the gunsight tail fin lights. Did he ever hit over sixty-five with you? Couldn't you feel the energy of the PowerFlite engine?"

I could tell by the smile on his face that Charles loves engines. He knows many facts about the Forward Look Chrysler vehicle— few adults know as much. Charles, like his father, has no interest in planes, but either of them could talk anyone into buying a car.

"Did Nonno ever take you over to Joe Rock's store on Warren Street?" Charles asks. "It was our favorite spot."

"Nope."

"He'd park his two hundred and twenty-six-inch flowing body sedan as effortlessly as slipping his hand into a glove. Once inside the store, he'd gab forever in Italian with Mr. Rock. He'd buy me warm roasted chestnuts. They talked while I ate." Charles licks his lips and rubs his belly. "Oh, and I can't forget the chunks of Parmigiana Reggiano cheese."

Charles always talks about food. As he inches toward the garden gate, he asks, "Did you try our neighbor Irene's prune tarts? Let's beat our feet and get upstairs."

"You go. I've got to check on some recent plantings in the garden for Nonnie. Don't eat everything."

Charles moves out. His arms look like a plane banking. His right arm is like one wing of the plane pointing toward the ground and the other arm to the sky. He moves faster. Now his movements are more like a football player running onto a field. He keeps his arms outspread and touches the top of every bush or flower as if greeting his football fans.

The garden gate slams shut behind him. I notice he enters the apartment through the side door of the garage. I bet he wants to inspect the chrome on the Chrysler.

I need to inspect and measure the progress of the newly planted items. Walking over to the opposite side of the garden, I look at the fall veggies.

My four-year-old brother, Freddy, sits near the rows of plantings playing with his cousins. Sweet Freddy gets along with everyone. He wears his favorite striped coveralls with the hand-sewn Texaco star over his heart. Today, he stayed home from the cemetery with a trusted sitter, Carl. They came over after the church service to hang out with cousins in the garden.

Carl has been an employee of Range Oil & Gas for many years. Sometimes he pitches in at the station, but mostly he enjoys coffee, naps, and watching us kids grow up. Carl is shorter than me, a kind man, and accommodating. He rarely expresses an opinion or talks.

Today, Carl keeps his eyes on the youngest group of kids. We all like him, and he doesn't snitch like Janie.

"Carl, no work today at the station? Did my mother get you to babysit again?"

"Right, Eugene, the station is closed 'cause your Gramps passed on. Sorry, you lost him. May he rest in peace. He lived to a ripe old age, and he's in a better place now."

This is a long speech for Carl. His kind words, however, leave me unexplainably edgy and irritated. My brother and cousins' whispering diverts my attention.

"What is it you're doing, Freddy?" I inquire.

He does not answer but looks toward our six-year-old cousin to respond. She tells me they are playing funeral. The hole and the rock covered with flowers all have meaning. I understand.

"Will I die when I take a nap, Carl? You know when I'm resting," asks Freddy fearfully.

"Oh, no," Carl replies. "You are way too young to die."

Too young to die? How can anyone say such a thing? Our baby Caesar came and went before Freddy's birth. This misunderstanding about aging and death cannot go unnoticed. I kneel by Freddy and take his hand. "Do you know how these plants started?" I ask.

"How does a plant grow?" he repeats and then replies, "They start when you open a package of seeds and put them in the ground."

I laugh to myself and agree. Plants start from seeds.

"Right, Freddy. A plant needs water. The right soil, sunlight, and seeds will begin a new life. Look around you. The plant grows and makes extra seeds. Then it's their time to die. Plants live and die like people. It's called the circle of life. It's nature; it's natural. Life goes on."

Freddy thinks about it and asks, "Did I begin as a seed?"

Carl and I look at one another, and we both chuckle. I need to put an end to this line of inquiry. "It's complicated. Ask Daddy about seeds and babies another day. He'll do a super-duper job of explaining." But I still have a point to clear up for Freddy. "Before you were born, we had another baby brother. He died, and we all cried. Then you were born, and we cried because we were happy."

"I'm glad I made everyone happy," says Freddy.

"You never forget someone who died. It's tough to understand now. No one has all the answers."

My wise words pleasantly surprise me. I hope a four-year-old can grasp some of it.

"So Nonno won't come back. He's not lost somewhere sleeping. He's not resting. He's dead," says Freddy innocently.

"And it's okay to be sad. We all love you. Talk to an adult if you have questions. Right, Carl?" I study Carl's face. Carl's wife died early in their marriage and left Carl with three boys to raise. He must have forgotten how children could get the wrong ideas about death and dying. Carl bows his head.

Freddy looks at me and says, "Bye, Eugene; we got rocks to bury here."

The fall plantings look good, especially the squash plants. Nonnie would not forgive me if anyone messed with her *fiori di zucca*. We seldom share her Italian fried flowers with non-Italians. The zucchini and pumpkin plants provided edible blossoms. But I wondered what Nonnie would say about the mysterious flower-topped mounds in her garden. Would she recognize it as a make-believe cemetery? Perhaps she would like the idea of her grandchildren replaying Nonno's funeral scene.

Nonnie's attitude about life comes from what she has experienced. She has learned to manage events in life as they came to her. She knows you cannot control everything, and she never trusts or puts her faith in luck. She has often told me there is always a choice, and laughing is better than crying.

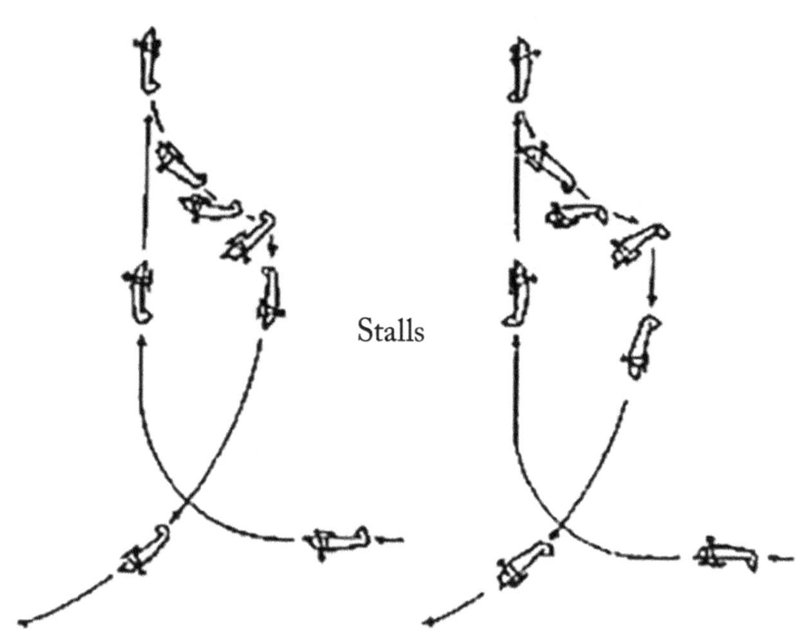

Stalls

Chapter 12

Visions of the crunchy, golden-brown fried zucchini flowers dance in my head. The squash plants will yield a delicious harvest, and my mouth drools in anticipation. As I walk toward the garden gate to go upstairs, someone calls my name.

I recognize my older cousin Carolyn's voice. She repeats my name as she nears the garden. "Eugene, I'm glad I found you." She pulls the garden gate open. Her wedding band gleams in the sunlight on the gate's handle. When she enters the garden, I notice she is carrying Nonno's Pendleton blanket. It is unbelievable to me. How did she get it? Carolyn motions me to follow her. As we arrive at the northern white cedar tree, she bends over and spreads out the blanket, smoothing out wrinkles and adjusting the fringe.

I still do not believe my eyes. This blanket has come from Nonno's car. Nonnie had wrapped it around his shoulders the night he died. Carolyn sits on it now.

"Eugene, whatever is wrong?"

My eyes remain glued to the blanket. Carolyn figures it out and explains, "I see you recognize Nonno's special blanket. Nonnie gave it to me and said she wanted me to have it because I'm their oldest grandchild. 'Keep it and dream of us giving you a warm hug on a cold night,' she said. Isn't it a comforting thought? I love this blanket."

Her words melt my annoyance a bit. I am pleased she has explained everything to me, and it makes me wonder if I will get a keepsake like this.

Carolyn babysat for us many years ago. Her mother and mine were sisters. Now my beautiful, clever cousin has a husband. We all like him, and not because of his bird-like whistling skills. Dean and

Carolyn were married in South Range, but then moved out of the area to work. She drove back for Nonno's funeral.

Soon Carolyn motions and invites all the other cousins to join us. She looks like a princess patiently awaiting her subjects. Little Freddy makes his way toward the blanket with Carl following. Soon everyone in the garden becomes part of her group. Carl decides it will be time for another cup of coffee since another adult is with the young ones. He leaves the garden and heads into the apartment.

"I'm pleased to see all of you. Come and sit," Carolyn says as she pats the blanket. She sits regally alone on the blanket. I keep my distance and stand still. The youngest sits on the grass.

"I'm going back home tomorrow," Carolyn begins, "but first, I wanted to talk to you about Nonno, the funeral, and your feelings. Sometimes it's hard to ask your parents questions."

We all exchange glances. Carolyn must be joking, right? Someone giggles. Everyone awkwardly waits for someone to answer her. After a long pause, ten-year-old Peggy asks her an unusual question.

"Why did he die?" Carolyn repeats. "You want to know what made Nonno die? Well, his liver stopped functioning. Another way of putting it is a part of his body didn't work anymore. Nonno had this problem for a long time, and his body just wore out."

Her matter-of-fact response astounds me. After all, it was not such a stupid question, and what a relief to learn the precise cause of Nonno's death. Everyone begins to feel comfortable and is eager to listen.

"I know some of you are too young, but those who are older," she looks directly at cousins over age eight and stops at me, "will remember today. You'll find out life passes too swiftly. Significant events like births, weddings, and watching kids grow up are the milestones."

"What's a milestone?" little Freddy asks. "Is it a stone, like an agate or sandstone?"

"No, they're not rocks or stones. Milestone is a word for important events in your life, like Nonno's funeral today. The funeral is a significant milestone, especially for your parents. Their pa died. Sometimes adults act mad or act differently during a sad time. They won't talk or share their feelings like we are now." Carolyn becomes still, inhales deeply, and places a hand over her heart. "Be extra kind to your mom or dad right now. Nonno, their pa, is gone. We have to understand their grief and what a sad time this is for them."

Freddy goes over and sits on Carolyn's lap.

"Don't be sad. I'm here," Carolyn says, hugging him.

Kathy raises her hand to get Carolyn's attention. "Is it okay to talk about Nonno?"

"Oh, yes, don't be afraid to say his name or talk about him. Let's talk about something special you remember about Nonno right now." She pauses, scans all our faces, and settles on me. "You begin, Eugene."

"Me?" I ask. Oh, how I hate when teachers pull that trick on me. Carolyn has put me on the spot. I heave my shoulders and begin to speak, relying on instinct. "I'm going to remember us flying his plane. Once, we flew over this garden. Nonno was like the noble gray owl that flies day or night, always flying low over the ground. He called me a peregrine falcon because I wanted to fly fast." I search my cousins' faces and ask, "Who's next?"

Carolyn's smile of approval pleases me. Now all the cousins start to chatter and come up with ideas.

"Remember, Nonno and the relatives gathered by the gas station on the Fourth of July? Didn't you enjoy sitting high on the red Texaco fuel delivery truck's walkway?" Bobby says. Everyone nods their head in agreement.

"You got to sit inside the truck, Bobby, with your father," reminds Ruth.

"Wasn't it fun tossing out candy to people on the street watching the parade?" Nancy chimes in. She does an imaginary toss of candy into her sister Jeanne's open mouth.

"I'm sure I ate more candy than I tossed," sweet Norma Jean admits, laughing.

"I will decorate a box and put in those cheery yellow daisies with the black centers." We all watch as Barb goes over and pulls on a flower. Betty scampers after her to help. Up comes the plant, roots and all. "When I see this flower, I'll remember our talk today."

Carolyn begins to speak but pauses. We both know those black-eyed Susans were Nonno's favorite flowers. The flowers in Nonnie's garden reminded him of the giant sunflowers he had seen in Italy. Carolyn never reprimands the flower picker.

Holding her folded newspaper clipping, Enid finally says, "I'm making a memory box and putting the newspaper articles of Nonno in it."

Mary Ellen stands there watching and listening. Now she raises her hand to ask a question. "Should I be afraid of dying?" She crosses both hands over her heart and waits for an answer.

Carolyn thinks for a minute and replies, "No one knows when they will die. But you are all young and healthy. Death makes life precious, so live and don't worry too much about it. Be safe. Work out things in your head about the choices you make. Luck is sometimes perfect and sometimes flawed."

Carolyn studies her gold ring as we absorb her words. She then opens her hands, palms facing up, and raises and lowers each one separately. It reminds me of a teeter-totter or an antique balance scale. She only says one word, "Choices."

Janie speaks in a whisper and asks. "Why can't people live forever? Why do people have to die?"

Carolyn's black eyelashes lower and close, and a tear appears on her cheek. "I, um, I don't have the answer for you. In my heart, I believe God knows when we will die. My faith provides me with peace and comfort." She inhales sharply, brushes aside the tear, and adds, "Don't be afraid of living. Things can change in an instant. So don't wait to tell someone how you feel. Sad to say, death is the only certain thing in life." She opens her arms, and all of my young cousins join her on the blanket for a group hug.

A warm feeling enters my heart, and I enjoy seeing my cousins on the blanket with Carolyn. I decide Nonnie made an excellent choice in giving Carolyn Nonno's blanket.

Janie taps me on the shoulder. "Heavy stuff," she says, "but it helps me understand why my dad is acting the way he is today."

Uncle Geno's behavior does need some explanation. I hope Janie can help him through this milestone in his life.

I doubt my mother and I will get into a "heavy" conversation like this. I remember once when we talked about death, and she laughingly said there was only one other certainty in life—taxes.

Carolyn gracefully gets up and refolds the blanket as Freddy points toward the vegetable section of the garden. Everyone follows him toward his make-believe cemetery.

Janie moves closer to me. "I got the message." She hugs me.

"Yeah," I say and step back to avoid her cooties. I stand alone and feel awkward and embarrassed. I need additional time to digest the emotional conversation. Charles should have heard everything as well.

I view Carolyn's heartfelt conversation to mean that life will not be like the popular TV show *The Adventures of Ozzie and Harriet*.

Everyone's troubles on that show are resolved with happy endings. Death does not seem appropriate, but it is the only certainty in life.

What has happened to Charles? He would have an opinion about all of this. I head toward the house to find him and perhaps more food.

Chapter 13

The street is still crowded with passing neighbors and friends. I imagine the kitchen table will have plenty of food, even those yummy prune tarts. Many visitors are entering through the main entrance, so I decide to go through the garage and use the back stairs like Charles. The gasoline smell welcomes me in the garage, and Nonno's car looks perfect in its usual spot. Charles' loving touch has provided the pristine shine.

As I start up the back staircase, I pause and study my shoes. The scuff marks set off warning bells.

"Consequences," says the dreaded inner voice. "Remember what you did this morning? Your actions will have consequences."

I sit on a stair and reflect on the day's events. Uncle Bruno left South Range only yesterday to pick up his brother Fred in Chicago. The timing in Chicago worked out perfectly, and they drove all night from the airport north to South Range. The funeral services were scheduled for nine o'clock in the morning. The family went to the church. However, the brothers were still on the road. Nonnie insisted the services not begin while her sons were missing. She refused to proceed without the presence of the entire family. The Holy Family Church reached capacity, and everything was in order. The church bells began to ring at nine o'clock, and Bruno and Fred miraculously arrived.

Someone had joked about how convenient it would have been if Nonno had died two weeks sooner. Uncle Fred and Aunt Chickie were in town from California at the time. It would have been easier than the sixteen hours of driving. Uncle Bruno had every reason to be tired after the long round-trip drive to Chicago. I hope to find Charles near the prune tarts, but it is understandable if his family left early.

I stand up and take the stairs two at a time, entering the busy multi-purpose room off the kitchen. Volunteers washed dishes, refilled platters, and kept the kitchen neat today. Someone calls out my name. Irene, our neighbor and a whirlwind of energy, recognizes me.

"Did you see your mom yet? She's asked me to watch out for you. Here, grab something to eat. I've saved a slice of Katie's povitica for you. You'll love it because there are lots of walnuts in it. And try my deviled eggs." She grins ear to ear. "You'll be needing 'angel eggs' after your mom gets her hands on you."

With my plate stacked with food, I move into the full-time kitchen. Conversations in English, Italian, and other languages create loads of chitter-chatter. Italians use their bodies when they talk, so I have to dodge hands and arms as my relatives gesture wildly. Bottles of homemade wine are on the counter. Although Nonno never drank, he always offered it to guests. Food and wine go together, and my grandparents were gracious hosts.

Uncle Fred, the eldest son, leans on the refrigerator, entertaining a couple of neighbors. He doesn't appear tired after his long trip from California, and his tanned face and intense eyes make him stand out in any group. Best of all, his lively style of storytelling fascinates me. I inch closer to him.

"It was 1919, and I disappointed Pa by telling him I hated flying, so he put me behind a steering wheel and told me to drive his buses. I'd sometimes work for fourteen hours straight. I was fine as long as my feet remained on the ground."

"I know you didn't like flying," a listener jokes, "but you saw lots of snow flying in the winter."

With a snort, Uncle Fred continues, "So Pa tells me if I'm not going to be a pilot, I gotta be the best bus driver. I ended up being one of his number-one mechanics, too. I went to study at Parks Air College back in 1928. Buses, planes, and trucks—I loved them all. You unfasten the hood, and those engines all look alike. Easy for me. I had to keep Ford's logging trucks moving during the war. We all know Michigan lumber built the gliders. The Waco CG-4As." He pauses to make sure his listeners agree, and he adds, "Kingsford had the factory."

"I worked in the Kingsford factory," a man says. "Our motto was 'make'um, and crate'um. Built more than any other company in the USA for the Army."

"Then you know what the letter 'G' stands for on the glider pilots' badge?" Uncle Fred asks.

This conversation sparks my curiosity more than a history lesson at school. I squeeze a little closer to the group. I would bet, like everyone else, the 'G' stood for the glider. I wait for him to agree.

Uncle Fred looks directly at the veteran glider maker. Like a celebrity, Uncle Fred divulges the answer. "The 'G' stood for gutsy." Uncle Fred is a natural showman. I find myself wanting to applaud. A woman nearby speaks up as we are all complimenting Uncle Fred on his story.

"Glider pilots? No, I'll tell you who I think deserved the 'G' for having lots of guts." Uncle Fred looks around for the unknown woman who has dared to interrupt and question his response. She is sitting at the table but gets up to join the men by the refrigerator.

She wears a formless black dress and carries a worn purse under her arm. Her gray hair reminds me of Nonnie's, but her face appears younger.

Uncle Fred tips his head in acknowledgment and respect for her. "Thank you for coming. How are you and your family?" Uncle Fred asks.

Without a smile or reply to his questions, she begins her own story in a heavily accented voice. "Imagine you're a Nazi in the German-occupied Soviet Union on a moonless night. Out of nowhere, you hear a 'whooshing' noise from above. Then there are the explosions—boom! The dark skies light up with bombings."

Uncle Fred nods his head, devouring her every word. She has us all under her spell. Our interest peaks as she counts to three with her fingers.

"Odin, dva, tri."

Fred counts along, "One, two, three."

"The Soviet Air Force female unit strikes once again. More come in flying at low altitudes. Again they cut the engine as they near their target. A sound, like a sweeping broom, is heard in the air. The women pilots drop the bombs, restart their motors, and depart. Gutsy women, yes?"

We all nod our heads in agreement and lean in to catch her every word. The foreign stranger goes on with her story.

"These gutsy and courageous women pilots were called Stalin's Hawks. The Germans feared and hated these Soviet Russian female bombers. Did you know what the Germans called us?"

"The Night Witches!" exclaims Uncle Fred. He shakes her hand and adds, "Thank you for the Soviet's support in the war, Marina. It made a tremendous difference, and the Night Witches earned three 'Gs' for their gallantry, grit, and guts."

"Incredible story," I say. "Were you one of those brave female pilots?"

She leaves the kitchen without replying. As my eyes follow her out of the room, I hear Uncle Fred say he has read that the "Night Witches" dumped 23,000 tons of bombs in 30,000 missions. Someone says Marina was a war bride. I wish I knew more about her—what a brave, mysterious woman.

Uncle Fred begins again. "Yup, talk about flying. Geno, Leo, and Norma liked flying with Pa. Ann, Bruno, and I enjoyed staying on the ground. And my hands were always greasy." He studies his hands, then asks, "Hey, speaking of my sisters, where are they?"

I had forgotten about my mother while listening to all these fascinating stories. Would she fly through the room like a witch on a broomstick looking for me? I decide it is time to make like a tree and leave.

As I pass by Uncle Leo, his hand presses on my shoulder and stops me. Uncle Leo and I are eyeball to eyeball. The palms of my hands sweat, and I hold my breath. He doesn't blink, and he doesn't speak. The waiting game has begun. Who will be the first to speak up?

Uncle Leo is the father of two young girls and knows all the tricks. We all love his warm-hearted manner, but he never lets much get by. I chew on my lower lip and see myself reflected in his eyeglasses. "Eugene, weren't you and Geno at the Sands today after the burial service?"

"Yes, who told you?"

He pauses to examine me before continuing, "I have so many memories of the Sands. I was probably ten or eleven years old when Pa sent me to work there. I trailed a railroad tie behind a vehicle to maintain the smooth landing strip. I was, in fact, younger than you. Our age made no difference. Pa never made you work hard, Eugene. In later years, he softened. So, why were you and Geno at the Sands?"

"What?" I ask, stalling for time. Uncle Leo doesn't appear to know about my cemetery exit story. Thankfully, a Finnish neighbor comes over and interrupts our conversation.

"Leo, you talking to da kid about da Sands airport? Caesar flew me over as one of the workers for the CCC. Off da Sands. Remember?"

"Eino, nice to see you. I didn't realize you were with the Civilian Conservation Corps?"

"Ya, da CCC gave us jobs after da Depression. Smart idea dat Roosevelt had. Mamma got twenty-two dollars every month in da mail. I got to keep eight. On da island, I planted trees—Dat's such a tiny island in huge Lake Superior. And I knew Caesar during da 1936–37 fire on Isle Royale. Ya, a burning island surrounded by da water."

"So," Uncle Leo says, "you knew Caesar during the big fire on Isle Royale. Water and flames everywhere and still an uncontrollable fire for months."

I had heard a lot about the fire on the island. I heard about Caesar flying supplies over there throughout summer and winter, but I never got many details.

Eino stops talking to light a cigarette. It fits the tale, but Uncle Leo and I know Nonnie does not like the smell of smoke in her house.

"Open the kitchen window," Uncle Leo tells me.

I stretch over the kitchen sink and yank. The window sash squeals like a piglet as it opens. I feel thankful my mother does not come to investigate the noise.

"Sorry, ya; it's a bad habit from da camp," says Eino. "Just wanna tell you how Caesar risked his life by flying from da Sands to the island. You know, during da fires. Finns would say he had 'sisu,' you know, guts. Oh, dat smoke, so bad, and such a heavy fog, like a whiteout in da snowstorm. Mr. Lucchesi was a fearless man. I admired him. Well, gotta go now. Sorry about your pa dying, Leo."

Uncle Leo and Eino shake hands, and I leave. My route through the living room does not get me far. Uncle Fred has left the kitchen and sprawls out in Nonno's favorite leather armchair. He waves me over. "Eugene, come sit by me. Nobody is going to tell Norma you're here."

"Don't do it," says the irritating cricket-like inner voice.

"Okay," I say as I hustle over and plop down on the carpeted floor next to him. I've sat at Nonno's feet and leaned against this chair several times before. Inside me, a peculiar combination of sorrowful and joyous sensations merge. I miss Nonno terribly, but listening to stories from his past helps me feel closer to him. The Lucchesi legend is alive.

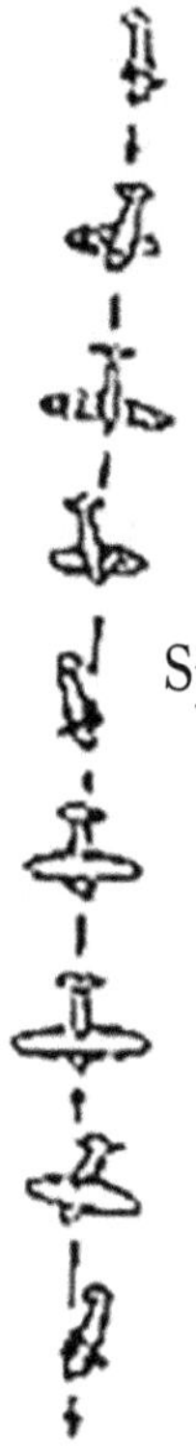

Spin

Chapter 14

Uncle Fred remains relaxed in the club chair with his large hands resting on the genuine leather armrests. He surveys the living room like a king and greets his subjects with a slight nod and a royal smile. Feeling like a humble servant or his favorite hunting dog, I nestle close to his feet and await his commands.

Other guests perch on Nonnie's fancy blue velvet sofa. Slowly, a serene calm settles over the room. All eyes turn to focus on Fred as we wait for King Fred to speak. His voice commands attention as he asks, "Anyone here want to confess they knew Harold Skelly?"

The mention of Skelly's name ignites the gathering. All around us, laughter erupts. Previously silent guests begin to elbow the person next to them. Another pioneering local pilot, Skelly triggers vivid memories.

"Fred, do you remember when Skelly parachuted out of the plane? He totaled your pa's plane." The speaker quickly makes the sign of the cross over his chest and looks upward.

It does not take long before another guy slaps his knee and says, "Remember in '31 when he and Wescoat had the Sikorsky flying boat service to Isle Royale off the Sands?"

"Could you ever forget those classy broads hired from New York City for the inaugural flight of the seaplane?" Some of the men in the room begin to hoot and holler while another one gives out a soft wolf whistle.

Like a monarch holding a scepter, King Fred lifts one hand and catches everyone's attention. The room becomes silent, and they wait for his majesty to speak.

"Gentlemen," he pauses, "please, don't say classy broads. They were classy Broadway showgirls." Everyone laughs.

Another fella says, "I recall that day. They were all musicians and named the Vincent Lopez Debutantes." King Fred gives this fella a royal nod of approval and then begins to talk.

"Yeah, Skelly piloted the Sikorsky S-38 for one summer. He flew Pa over to the island in it. What an amazing set of pilots. Ma liked Pa as her pilot, best of all. Remember Skelly took her up that Fourth of July and did three loop-the-loops. Looping the loops in the sky wasn't for her. She'd only ride with Pa after that."

King Fred thinks it necessary to demonstrate what three loop-the-loops look like, so he raises his right hand vertically and creates a circle. Then he raises his hand higher for the second loop and stands to finish the third and highest loop. "Skelly knew the sweet spot for the pull—not too hard, not too soft. It's one of the most complex aerobic maneuvers. You try it someday with a paper airplane."

King Fred settles back into his throne and revs his engines for fresh storytelling. "Norma remembers flying as a kid with the two of them. She started at three or four years old and could fit in front of Pa. She said it was scary, and she hung on tight when flying upside down in his bi-planes."

Uncle Fred rules the room now. Why did he have to use the word Norma? Of course, it reminds me that I still have not seen my mother, but his aviation stories are something I could share with her. I stay, and he starts another tale.

"Every chance they had, Skelly and Pa flew—even at night. Do you recall how they welcomed in a new year by flying? Left the Sands in 1931 and returned fifteen minutes later in 1932. Remember, they buzzed over the powerful light beam on the Hotel Scott in Hancock. Anyone here at the hotel's New Year's Eve Party that night?"

"You spinning stories again, Fred?" his brother Leo asks as he enters the room. The brothers clearly love each other's company. Heads turn like at a tennis match to watch the brothers as the two talk.

"Speaking about Skelly," says Leo, "did you know he got an important job as a commercial pilot with American Airlines before his duty in the war? He became our Major Harold J. Skelly, Air Transport Command pilot." Nobody says a word and Leo continues.

"Remember when Skelly died? It happened during the war, but not because of a bullet or plane crash. Some disease got him in '43. He died in England. Pa always called Skelly his war hero." Leo knows a bit about war. He served as a first lieutenant in World War II and the Korean War.

Additional guests join the Lucchesi brothers in the living room. Newcomers are forced to stand. I have never seen so many people jammed into a room before.

"Getting an earful, Eugene?" asks Uncle Leo.

"Leave the kid alone. It's a history class," Uncle Fred replies. He pats me on my head.

"Do you brothers remember the Royce brothers?" someone asks.

I want to hear more about the famous Royce brothers. I hope my good fortune will continue and my mother will not storm into the room.

"You can't imagine the amount of history with those two guys," Uncle Leo says. "The younger brother, Don, ended up in the Navy as a rear admiral and Ralph was in the US Army Air Force as a major general. We can be proud of our locally grown American heroes."

"All those medals they earned in World War II," some fellow adds, "the brothers deserve more than getting a road named after them in Hancock and Ripley." Heads bob up and down in agreement. I love my local history class lesson and feel like part of the group.

"So which brother earned the Distinguished Flying Cross, Eugene?" asks Uncle Leo.

"Huh?" All eyes focus on me. Everyone laughs at the inside joke. Now I feel as though I have failed the class.

"Leave the kid alone," Uncle Fred gently scolds.

Wives start to seek out their husbands. Each points to her watch, and like magic, the husband stands, bids his goodbye, and leaves. Fred shifts in his chair. The crowds thin as he yawns.

"Come on; one more story, Fred. Then I gotta go," a fellow on the sofa begs.

Fred thinks and says, "Leo, look at me. You know I never wore glasses like you and Bruno. Did you ever go to Dr. McClure in Laurium for your eyeglasses?"

Leo nods but remains quiet.

Uncle Fred shares the events of a serious plane crash. The story starts with Dr. McClure's cross-country plans using his Bonanza plane. He shares how the doctor and two others went to test the directional gyro. The dramatic end occurred when the plane slammed into the hangar, killing two of the three occupants. Uncle Fred concludes his story by saying, "God rest their souls."

The sad story changes the festive atmosphere in the living room. More folks leave to go to their homes. Uncle Leo comes over and sits closer to us, so close I notice dark circles under his swollen eyes. The brothers sigh in unison. The day's events have taken a toll on everyone.

Uncle Fred leans nearer to his brother and says, "You know, Leo, I'm the oldest of Pa's sons. Maybe not his ideal son because he never taught me to fly like you. But he knew I worked hard and did my best. That's what Pa wanted us to do. We didn't have the comforts our kids have now."

They hesitate, and I comment, "You guys and Nonno accomplished lots. We've got Toro snowblowers, television sets for news, and even a vaccine for polio. Life isn't as difficult as in your olden days."

"The kid's honest," says Uncle Leo. "Pa was hard on us, and times have changed, but Pa always treated everyone equally. Today at church, rich mining bosses and poor farmers came to honor him. Pa was a legend in his own time."

Their voices lower, thick with emotion. I stay at Uncle Fred's feet, eager to hear more.

"We know Pa wasn't a religious person. Ma did all the church stuff. The priest today upset me. Ah, maybe I was tired from the drive up, but he seemed to judge Pa 'cause he wasn't in church every Sunday. Look how Pa felt about people and gave them a chance, even a second chance."

"I hear you, brother. Yeah, Pa taught us to be grateful Americans. We're living off his fame and fortune now. Lucky we still got his co-pilot Ma. Remember when they'd sing their song about flying? Flying away to a land, a place where joy would never end. Pa's first to depart to that land."

The brothers move their heads closer together and begin to sing softly. My position on the floor places me in the center of them. I recognize the tune. I heard Nonno hum it on the plane.

Our circle of closeness comes to an abrupt stop when someone shouts from the other side of the living room, "Geno is here!"

The backlight from the kitchen outlines his body. He appears like a super-sized giant posed to attack. Uncle Fred and Uncle Leo stop their singing and stare.

Flying-on-Edge

Chapter 15

The dramatic arrival of Uncle Geno pleases everyone except me. The group in the living room practically applaud at the sight of the three Lucchesi brothers together.

My reaction is different. Hot saliva fills my mouth as my gut clenches. The sour taste of deviled eggs climbs into my throat and threatens a violent ejection. I choke back a colorful disaster and know my extended procrastination time limit has terminated.

"I've been looking for you," Uncle Geno says. His dark eyes bore into me like poison-tipped spears. My body begins to go numb from the imagined poison.

"A pleasure to see you," greets a neighbor. "You've missed some marvelous aviation stories. You got one to contribute? How about we finish on a high note with a celebration at Laurium Airport?"

"No crashes, please," says another neighbor.

It is unthinkable for Uncle Geno to refuse an opportunity to tell a story. He steps into the living room but stands at a distance from us. From my position on the floor, Uncle Geno appears larger than life. I feel like a pesky cockroach ready to be crushed. He takes his eyes off of me and glances at his audience. The thumping of my head matches the pulsing of my heart. I fear what might happen next.

Uncle Geno starts his story, and my luck continues. "I remember the 1950 air show in Laurium, the same airport as the McClure crash, but a different year."

He pulls his gaze away from me and begins telling a story I have heard before. My gaze remains locked on the floor, and I listen.

"Pa flew against Reverend Schick and competed in the spot landing contest." Uncle Geno uses all the correct aviation terms. "First-place wins always went to Pa. Don't race against the Lord's representative, Ma told him. Pa did it anyway. He blamed Ma's prayers for the outcome. Reverend Schick didn't lose, and neither did Pa—it was a tie." Geno waits for the laughter to stop.

Now I see the Uncle Geno I know. He woos us all with a contagious wide grin and a twinkle in his eye. My lips form into a small smile. His storytelling defuses my situation.

He continues with the story. "My turn came in the program. I demonstrated how not to fly a Piper Cub. Ma was always worried. You know I'd done this event at many shows before. She firmly insisted Pa drive her into town. Ma thought her prayers might go unanswered. She'd rather buy a hat than watch the stunt."

"Geno, landing without power is always dangerous. Trying to earn a 'G' for gutsy?" Uncle Fred asks.

"He finds pleasure in performing this dead stick landing," says Uncle Leo.

"True, if you're like me and know what you are doing," says Uncle Geno. "No power, the prop stops, it's kaput, thus the dead-stick landing. The spectators get a thrill out of it. Pa always greeted me with a handshake, and it made him proud to see me succeed."

"Better than the alternative—a crash," says Uncle Fred. "You'd make Ma mad then. She's usually calm, but light her up the wrong way and—boom. She's a firecracker. You know Norma is the additional one who is the emotional Italian?"

"Remember the air show when Pa saw his first jet aircraft?" says Uncle Leo. "Only three years ago, he knew he was too elderly to learn to fly one. We watched them fly overhead, and oh, boy, he wanted to do a barrel roll in one. Pa loved flying—what a pilot."

I correct him, speaking up without fear. "Nonno was exceptional," I stop for emphasis, "an outstanding aviator," I add proudly.

Some folks in the room grin and nod their heads. My three uncles react differently. They focus their attention on me. Uncle

Geno takes a step back into the kitchen and motions for me to follow him. There are no cries of protest from Uncle Leo or Uncle Fred to leave me alone. I stand and head toward the kitchen alone. My legs must have fallen asleep because I almost drop. I force myself not to tumble and will myself to walk.

"Ma and your mother want to see you immediately. They know you're here. I'm escorting you to their bedroom door now. Your time for hiding is over."

"Tick, tick, tick, tick," sings the annoying inner voice.

Looking at Uncle Geno, I confidently say, "I'm glad you picked me up at the Sands today. But my mother said I could go. She knew where I was going."

"She told you to go?"

"Yes, my mother noticed me watching the plane. She knew what I thought. She understood," I add with conviction, "She told me to go. I read her lips, g-o, Uncle Geno."

He shakes his head in disbelief. Uncle Geno shocks me with the truth. "Eugene, I heard her say no, n-o."

We both stop outside of the bedroom door. My mouth hangs wide as I consume this news. I spent all day under the impression she understood my inner turmoil. She never read my mind or understood. Now I cannot focus on this upsetting piece of information. How could one two-letter word make such a world of difference? I deserve punishment, and I have earned my mother's wrath.

This day has turned out to be the worst of my life. I have defied my mother, acted selfishly, and brought shame to the family. I want my bones to disintegrate, my body to collapse, melt, and disappear. I long to be nothing. I cannot face her.

Uncle Geno glares at me and says, "Get in there now."

"But it's so quiet, Uncle Geno. Maybe they're all sleeping."

He pushes open the bedroom door. Then he forces me through the open doorway with a not-so-gentle nudge.

The bright lights of the kitchen create a contrast to the softly lit bedroom. My eyes adjust, and I study Nonnie seated in the chair. Her eyes are closed and her shoes off. It looks like she holds a rosary in her hands. Aunt Ann stands squeezed between the chair and wall and rubs her shoulders. They are still wearing their funeral clothes from earlier today. Nonnie's favorite bottle of Coty perfume leaves a floral hint of roses in the bedroom.

Another figure stands by the window. With another not-so-gentle shove from Uncle Geno, the lights from the kitchen disappear as the bedroom door closes. Click. My body vibrates, and my shoes act like magnets. They keep me attached to the floor. I cannot flee.

"Times up," says the smug inner voice with satisfaction.

My eyes adjust to the soft bedroom light. The dark figure of a woman moves toward me from the window. It advances, and I recognize it as my mother.

She comes closer and speaks in a whisper. "Finally, we're together, Eugene. I've waited all day to see you. I didn't want you to go to bed before I talked with you."

As she approaches, I stand there terrified. What will the next several minutes bring? Today's crazy conduct demands that I receive punishment.

I see her puffy eyes as she nears. The two extra women in the room decrease into specks in the background. My mother's face enlarges as she comes within inches of my face. I can smell the cheese on her breath as she speaks.

"At the cemetery this morning, things went wrong between us when the plane flew by. I should have hugged you instead of screaming the word 'no' at you."

I begin, "You didn't say 'go'? But I thought—" I do not finish my sentence. What has made me evade her all day long? A two-letter word?

"I'm your mother, the adult, and to get angry at you was a dangerous mistake. I'm so sorry I acted without thinking. Being mad is how some of us handle sadness. It's not the fitting way."

I start to speak. "I'm sorry, too."

"Stop," she interrupts. "It's in the past. Let's fix this problem together. Would you like to go back sometimes to the Sands with me? We can talk about Nonno."

My pain of grief, fear, and misunderstanding decrease. Why have I wasted energy and time today to avoid my mother?

"Will the pain ever go away when you lose someone you love?" I ask.

She wraps her arms around me and spells out the answer. I hear the two-letter word correctly this time. With a light kiss on my cheek, she makes her final request. "Son, please forgive me. I'm sorry; I'm sorry."

"The airplane is the closest thing to real magic
that we have."
—Charles Lindbergh

Part III
July 2020

AUTHOR'S NOTES

Attention readers—as you begin the final descent into the remaining portion of your book, please make sure you are aware of the following facts: You may proceed into Part III and return to this information below or continue reading and take note of the author's use of truth and fiction.

ALERT Fact & Fiction *ALERT*

Eugene's experience with John Sessions' crew, Colonel Hamilton, and Colonel Halvorsen's meetings happened as stated. Other historic notable aviators mentioned did and do exist. Caesar's 1932 trip to the Cleveland Air Races and his photo taken of the Powder Puff derby aviatrixes are real. The Wall of Fade, lined with Lucchesi photographs, new and old, is accurate, too.

Please keep in mind that the author has tampered with the truth. The conversation between the family at the summer home, Apollo the dog, the Terran family, their history, and their meeting is fiction.

On behalf of the publisher, author, and the entire Lucchesi crew, we appreciate you for choosing us on this flight into the past. We look forward to hearing from you in the future.

"When everything seems to be going against you,
remember that aircraft take off against the wind,
not with it."
—Henry Ford

The Wall of Fade

WHO'S ON THE WALL OF FADE?

1. Leo, Bruno, and Geno

2. Caesar and Jennie

3. Caesar

4. Norma

5. Leo

6. Fred and Jennie

7. Ann, Baby Norma, Martina

8. Caesar and Bruno

9. Jennie and Norma

10. Jennie

11. Norma and Lindy

12. Jennie and Eugene

13. Cleveland Air Race Aviatrixes

1
2
3
#1 Plane
COTT
JOHNSON OIL REFINING CO
KANT-NOCK ETHYL GASOLINE
4
6
5

Who Wanns
Some Gas?
8
7
SAMMY MASON
9
10
12
11
"Pals"
and Lindy
13
Cleveland

"Fiction is the truth inside the lie."

—Stephen King

Chapter 16

"Sorry," a distant voice says. "I'm sorry to disturb you, Gramps."

I jerk up and recognize my granddaughter Angelina's voice. The reality of today's events confronts me—it is 2020, not 1957, and I'm no longer a growing lad.

"Everyone has been looking for you. Finding you in bed is the last place I thought you'd be. Are you all right? I overheard you mumbling, and you repeated the words no, no. A nightmare? I can't believe you were dozing off." She looks at me intently. "Napping isn't your thing, Gramps."

Angelina takes out her cell phone and texts a message. "I'm informing the others you're in bed, not working in the back garage. We were worried about you. You disappeared after the long phone call." Angelina places a hand on my forehead, checking my temperature. "No fever; you're okay. We've got guests coming. It's not a joke. Come on; get up."

"In a minute," I reply. "Let me clear my head." I am waving my hand to shoo Angelina away. I glance at the bedroom dresser. Sitting on top is a framed picture of my parents. "Thanks for the journey down memory lane," I address the photo as I sit up.

"You're mumbling again," Angelina says and walks off to the kitchen.

I sit in bed, remembering the mystery caller discussing Nonno's funeral and the day I had forgotten. I bend over to put on my shoes and continue going over the call earlier this morning with a sigh. It had to have triggered the dream and buried memories. Having someone write a school history paper about me felt like an invasion of privacy, which disturbed me. Were they aware of everything? What else did they know about the other major events in my life? Flopping back into the bed, I recall two additional significant incidents from the 1950s.

The first involved a specific airline. Specifically, the airline's 4:30 p.m. flight from the Houghton County airport that transported me to a hospital hundreds of miles away and saved my life. It happened in '58, a year after Caesar's death.

The school year had ended and summer begun. As a teenage boy with lots of energy, I needed to work, so Uncle Geno suggested I help out at the South Range gas station. My primary duties were to greet customers with a smile and clean their windshields.

One July afternoon, another employee came to cut grass near the fuel storage tanks. I was clearing the area, gathering twigs, soda bottles, and paper not far from where he was running the rotor-powered lawnmower.

That is when it happened. I bent over to pick up a piece of wood. I stood and felt an enormous pain in my back. The lawnmower moved away from me, making loud noises as it spit out grass, rocks, and debris. I could not figure out what had happened. Nobody was nearby, but my back felt like a truck had slammed into me.

The worker continued mowing and passed by me without any concern. However, when he looked and saw the strained expression on my face, it frightened him. He asked, "What happened?"

I shrugged my shoulders and could not answer. The man left me and finished the mowing. Any movement in my back caused severe pain. It became difficult to breathe. Frightened, I turned to head into the office. My mother was working as a bookkeeper that day. I needed to talk to her fast. I stumbled into the office feeling dizzy and lightheaded.

She was on a phone call and did not notice me. I clutched the end of her desk to keep from falling. My voice only came out as a whisper. Finally, she glanced at me, and her mouth fell open as she cried with alarm. She slammed the phone down.

Unable to speak, I used my hands and pointed to my back. Tears began to well up in my eyes from pain and fear. She sat me in her chair, then left the office to find help and learn what had happened.

Everyone she questioned had the same answer. No one knew what had happened. My breathing became difficult, and my lips began to turn blue. She got me in the car and raced to the doctor's office. It proved to be useless. The doctor was not there. My mother drove over the bridge to the emergency room at the local hospital. My symptoms kept getting worse. A visiting physician examined me. He advised my family to rush me to the Duluth Clinic—over two hundred miles away. A flight might save my life. That is when North Central Airlines came to the rescue.

This accident happened many years ago, and Dr. Fuller performed a miracle operation. He removed a two-inch piece of wire that had sliced through my lung and lodged against my spine. The blades of the lawnmower had powered this projectile. It was a tiny metal sliver that barely left a scratch upon entering the skin on my chest, but it had acted like a bullet. An x-ray discovered the piece. The surgery left a foot-long scar like a shark's bite under my arm for a lifetime. I survived, and it didn't prevent me from landing my first commercial copilot position with that airline in 1973. The airline's name later changed with new ownership, but I stayed loyal to the company throughout my flying career.

Following my lawnmower incident, another flight played an essential part in changing my life. Nonnie and I traveled to Italy in 1959. Our captain let me into the cockpit on the international leg of the journey.

I could not believe my eyes when the compartment door
opened, and the instrument panels glowed like a box of jewels. I was
full of endless questions, and the flight crew loved my enthusiasm
and knowledge about flying. That moment clinched my desire to stay
in aviation. As a fifteen-year-old boy, I knew flying was in my blood.

"Gramps, where are you? Get out here!" Angelina yells from the
kitchen.

I get out of bed with a mighty heave. I smile as I return my gaze
to the photo of my parents on the bureau. Maybe there is a historical
account to be told after all. I need to appreciate my ancestry. They
did leave a legacy of fliers behind.

Walking into the kitchen, I tell myself to put memories
aside and focus on chores. I do not count on the three vacationing
grandkids for too much help. Their traditional reunion to our
Michigan home from various other regions is a welcomed break. The
cousins are old enough to travel alone, and their working parents love
the break. The summer of COVID-19 brings risks, and I hope our
safe practices keep us virus-free, healthy, and alive.

Living on the Portage Canal allows you to have fun in a
beautiful setting. Growing up in South Range was great as a
youngster, but my parents believed a house on the water would
bring their five adult children and grandkids back home. They were
correct—we still come back.

Chapter 17

My folks have been dead for several years. I acquired their lakefront house and took care of refurbishing it both inside and out. When guests visit, I appreciate it when they identify the house's original features that I chose to maintain. Many people have commented on how beautifully we mixed the old and new. Family members live in different parts of the country, but we all enjoy the history and relaxed atmosphere in Michigan's Upper Peninsula. Plus, there's always something to do with so many local relatives. The Copper Country will always be home.

Being a retired pilot with pass privileges allows me to visit the old homesite on the water frequently. And I consider myself fortunate to fly my private single-engine plane across the nation to Houghton County. The Peter Pan in me seems to need freedom.

This morning's phone conversation reminded me of my childhood with my grandparents. As I remember Nonno's funeral services, a stab of sadness pierces my heart like an icicle. That discussion reawakened feelings I had buried the day he was buried. I never considered stepping into his shoes or following in his footsteps. As a businessman, my grandpa Caesar Lucchesi was ahead of his time. He was a hero to me.

How could someone think I am a hero and worthy of a story? A chuckle escapes from my throat as I remember how I avoided my mother all that day, g-o versus n-o—a stupid mistake. In the end, she acted like an adult, which drew us closer together. My calm father and lively mother assisted me in comprehending my grandfather's passing. As a child, it was difficult. It's still tough as an adult. Missing someone you care about will always be painful.

The sound of giggling and voices from around the house return me to the present, and I search for the box of surgical face masks. Because of the terrifying pandemic, we will all be washing our hands and wearing masks during the summer of 2020. This awful illness is like a thief, robbing families of their lives and creating troubles worldwide. My religion keeps me hopeful, but the virus appears to be getting worse rather than better this summer.

I grab my blue face mask. It takes me a second to recognize the two masked adults as the voices get closer. My first impulse is to rush over and embrace my cousin Betty, who is ten years younger. Instead, we exchange nods and elbow bumps. She receives a bump on each elbow since she's related. Betty's smiling eyes twinkle a welcome as I say hello to her husband.

"Welcome, Betty and Mark. I'm glad you're masked. I'm over seventy-five and trying to live forever." I laugh at myself. I share my favorite current COVID quote with them. "It was better in the seventies when we were in our twenties than today in the twenties when we're in our seventies."

Betty's muffled laugh escapes her mask. She is many years my junior.

I lead them down the freshly mowed lawn to the lakeshore. We gaze at the picture-perfect blue sky and the white sand on our small beach. The sunshine warms our skin, and the sound of the gentle lapping waves is so relaxing that nobody speaks. We stand there, enjoying the pure, fresh Michigan air.

Eventually, Betty breaks the silence. "Don't you love the smell of cut grass?" she asks.

The words that come out of my mouth surprise me. "No, it reminds me of Caesar's funeral in the cemetery back in 1957."

"The funeral was over sixty years ago, Eugene. It's funny you brought it up. We went to see Charles. He showed us images and gave me a newspaper story about Caesar's funeral. Charles said it was a big deal in town. He also told me you'd want to forget the day. Charles said there was some strange story about the Sands and Uncle Geno. What's it all about?"

"Hey, is this a conspiracy or what? I just got off the phone with someone asking me about Caesar's funeral. Who's playing jokes on me? Did Charles put you up to this? It's not funny."

Mark and Betty's questioning eyes search out each other, and an uncomfortable silence surrounds us.

"Weird, this is too weird," I say. Changing the subject, I ask, "How about something to drink?" I spot my two granddaughters nearby. "Girls, hustle up some refreshments from the house and bring them to us elders out on the dock." No one moves toward the house. "Please," I add.

"Oh, don't bother," says Betty. "Mark and I came out here to visit you for a short time and ask you about your experiences last summer with the D-Day 75th Anniversary event. Mark was in the Air Force for six years and loves aircraft and aviation history. Do you have time for a story or two?"

Bijou, my granddaughter visiting from the East Coast, comes over to me and rubs my back. She intuitively knows the phone call and cemetery talk bothered me. Her French father named her correctly—she is a jewel. Bijou tells Mark I am a docent at the Museum of Flight in Seattle. She proudly praises my passion for sharing aviation with the public.

"Grandpa-O," she loves using this term of endearment with me, "let's go to the deck by the house. We can sit outside in the shade, enjoy our view of the water, and check out the famous Wall of Fade inside the house."

As we stroll up the grassy slope, Mark asks from behind his mask, "What is a Wall of Fade?"

Horizontal Circle

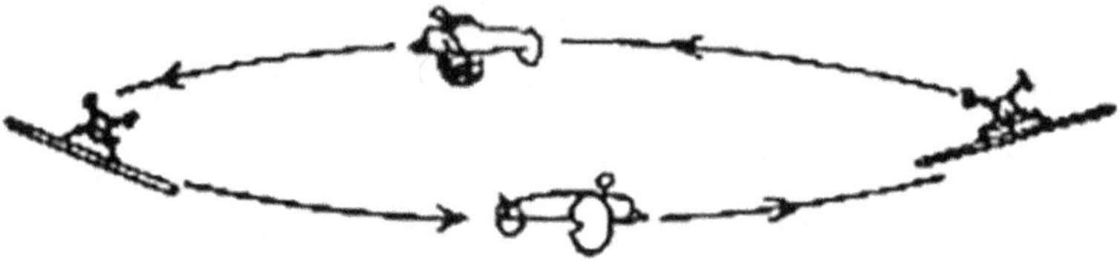

Chapter 18

A sliding door leads into a screened porch from the house's outside decking. One interior wall is devoted to family photos my parents arranged long ago. Although years of sunlight have faded the images, I leave the museum-worthy antique framed prints up in their honor. The once sharp pictures and features of the photographs are becoming dimmer with time.

"This is our Wall of Fade," I say, pointing to the vast assortment of photographs.

Betty and Mark look at the wall. "Wow, I can certainly understand why you call it the Wall of Fade. The sunlight has worked its magic here," Betty says, laughing. "You can barely recognize some of them."

She points out and starts listing the names of relatives. "Oh!" she says after patiently browsing through the images. "Look, Mark, there's one of my father." She points to a photo of Uncle Bruno standing between our Uncle Leo. She jumps excitedly and points to the large oval picture from the early 1900s.

"Look, the wedding picture of Caesar and Jennie. Can you believe they eloped? She was sixteen, and he was twenty-six. They spent a lifetime together in the air and on the ground."

"You knew these people, Betty?" Bijou asks.

"Their wedding happened over a century ago. They were your grandparents, but not mine."

Betty and the rest of us stare in total disbelief. Bijou notices and corrects herself, "I mean, they were my great-great-grandparents. Ernie and Norma are my great-grandparents."

"Your family is rich in history," Mark replies. "The Wall of Fade is quite impressive." He points toward numerous pictures and asks his wife for stories.

"All right, hubby, here are the highlights on the wall." She starts explaining as she points to the framed photo in the center. We all follow her finger and strain to hear her words. "Okay, Mark, look

at Caesar next to his new plane in 1931. And this is Eugene's mother, Norma, with her hand on the Piper Cub's wooden propeller. She's sixteen and completed her first solo flight. Look over there. This picture shows Leo standing next to a Monocoupe airplane. Did Leo get a pilot's license?"

I have to think a minute, then reply, "Yes, in the late thirties before World War II."

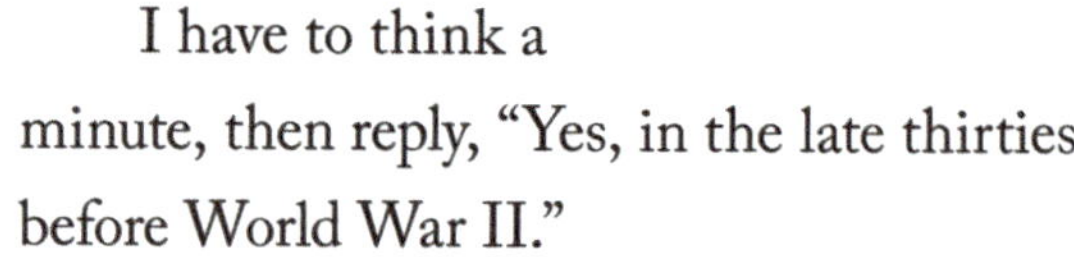

"And up there," Betty says, "see the oldest brother Fred wearing his Cloverland Transit bus driver uniform

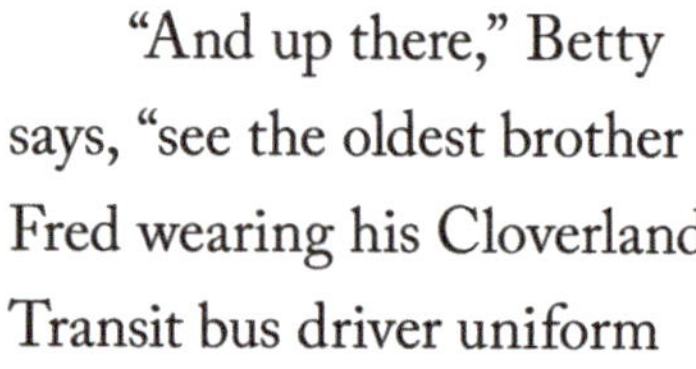

in 1937. Taxi, bus lines, airplanes—I told you Caesar was a pioneer in transportation."

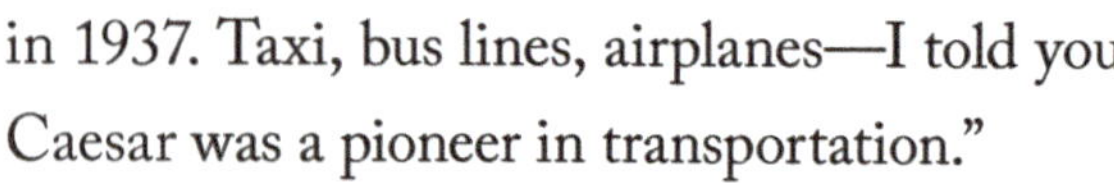

Mark's eyes roam across the Wall of Fade and devour every picture. He turns to me and states, "Caesar, his children, and you have all been attracted with flight. Three generations of fliers become pretty outstanding."

"Correction," says his wife. "Caesar's great-granddaughter also got her pilot's license at age seventeen. I'm talking about our cousin Robert's daughter, Jill."

"Yes," I agree and look at Betty. "Caesar got us off the ground, and his legacy is four generations of flying."

Betty and the girls loudly discuss one particular photo. Bijou shares her knowledge of the family by telling them the baby in the 1923 picture is their great-grandmother, Norma. The older woman holding her is Norma's older sister, Ann. She looks mature enough to be Norma's mother. Ann is leaning against a hand gas pump by the Lucchesi apartment garage on First Street in South Range. "Hey, here's one of my father, Bruno. It's the framed picture with Caesar standing shoulder-to-shoulder in front of the Texaco station. It's my dad, Bijou, and I know him very well," she adds to tease my granddaughter about her earlier mistake.

Mark motions to a black-and-white photograph. "I believe I recognize Mrs. Caesar Lucchesi in this photograph. It appears to be an air show. Is that Norma, the young woman, standing next to her? And who exactly is Sammy

Mason? See," he says, tracing his finger across the lettering painted on the plane's side. "Sammy Mason."

"The name seems familiar, but the Sammy Mason I know now competes on the Red Bull air racing circuit. I'll look into the name and see if there's a family history of flying."

As I search for my favorite picture, we all soak in the memories like the photographs absorb other UV rays, fading history's physical evidence. I point to the black-and-white photo that is aging and shrinking.

"Oh, there it is. Here's the picture I took of Nonnie. You kids never got to eat in her kitchen in South Range—the one above the garage. Remember those spaghetti cousin meals, Betty? Nonnie always wore an apron and made you sample everything she cooked."

"Wish I were at her kitchen table now," says Sonny. "What's there to eat?"

"Sonny, we still make some of her favorites. In a way, she's still feeding us," Bijou responds. "Her spaghetti sauce recipe is Gramp's specialty."

Betty begins to laugh. "Charles loves to cook too, and his gatherings are always grand. Which reminds me, we promised to visit him today. But before we leave, will you tell Mark a bit about your D-Day flight experiences from last summer?"

Sharing stories about my flying history is enjoyable; however, the call this morning is still bugging me. I have a question for Betty. "Sure, but first you must tell me if Charles requested someone call and interview me about flying. It isn't easy to think that someone is interested in my life. So, did Charles plan this prank?"

She does not answer and instead continues to ask questions. "Why don't you feel you made history like Caesar, Eugene?" She places her hand on my shoulder and says, "Are you too humble?"

"If you're fortunate to choose a job you love," Mark pipes up, "you never have to work a day in your life."

"He got the saying out of a fortune cookie," laughs his wife.

"Confucius is right. My years of flying as a commercial pilot satisfied my passion for aviation. Today, the individual on the telephone hinted about their devotion to the sky, too. It is hard to believe some other person lives and breathes flying like Nonno and I did."

Angelina pipes up and asks, "What do you know about the unknown caller?"

"The voice sounded like a kid's. I'm still unsure whether it's a growing boy or a girl. They did tell me their name and age, but I didn't catch it. You walked into the kitchen, Angelina, at that time."

I take a step toward her and add, "It's not your fault my hearing isn't as good as it used to be. They did mention the Young Eagle program. Remember when you were involved with them, Sonny?"

"Yes, I participated in the Young Eagles program and got a free airplane ride with them. It must have been when I was about eleven. They're part of the group out of Oshkosh. It's great when kids from eight to seventeen can get a free ride in an airplane."

My docent training kicks in, and I add a few additional details that Sonny has overlooked.

"Sonny, the Experimental Aircraft Association, or EAA, is headquartered in Oshkosh. We enjoy the huge air shows there. The EAA promotes and motivates children to learn about aviation, and Young Eagles is the ideal option."

"But back to your phone call, Eugene. Did your caller have a background in flying?" Betty asks.

"Yes, they mentioned they were accumulating flying hours."

"It must be a boy. Girls don't want to be aviators," says Sonny.

We laugh as his cousins walk over and pound him on the arms and back in mock horror. "I'm just kidding," he adds, attempting to defend himself.

"Well," I tell them, "the joke will end later today. I want you to join me when it's time to meet our mystery aviator." Suddenly, my grandkids come up with an excuses why they can't go. I raise my hand in the middle of the commotion and say, "No excuses, kids. Mark, it's time to share a story about my D-Day 75th Anniversary flying experience. Do you want to hear a sweet story or a story about a daring flight over enemy territory?"

"Why aren't there photos of you and the 2019 D-Day Anniversary?" Mark asks as he points to the Wall of Fade. "You have a flying history like Caesar. He'd recognize those planes."

"Good idea, Mark," I reply and watch my disinterested grandkids wander off and disappear like evaporated dewdrops on the lawn. Mark, Betty, and I make ourselves comfortable on the wooden chairs on the deck.

"So, is it a sweet story you want or one about flying over enemy territory?" I ask again.

Betty's eyes light up with approval, and Mark answers, "Both stories, Eugene, please."

Chapter 19

"I'll try not to bore you with too much information, Mark. Our docent training emphasized keeping your story brief so you don't lose your audience. Don't be polite. Give me a signal to 'decrease my story' and 'increase telling speed,' okay? I'm also famous for wandering off on tangents."

"Eugene," Mark quickly responds, "remember I've spent six years in the Air Force and am greatly interested in aircraft. I'm eager to hear all about your D-Day adventure. Let's take off."

Betty and Mark make themselves comfortable as I begin telling about the anniversary of recognizing those who died during battles over Normandy in World War II.

"It was an honor to relive history beside a living legend. Colonel David Hamilton is the last Pathfinder pilot still alive. This year celebrates the seventy-fifth anniversary of his journey over the English Channel. Imagine being twenty-one in 1944 and flying airborne parachuters over enemy territory."

"Stop," says Betty raising her hand. "I need to know about World War II before you move on. Of course, I'm aware of the Big Three—the United Kingdom, the Soviet Union, and the United States. Those three countries were the Allies who stood up to the Axis powers of Germany, Japan, and Italy. So, on D-Day in 1944, the Allies planned to stop Hitler with a massive, united invasion of France. Mark, am I on the right track? Eugene?"

"Yep, that's right—that longest day was June 6, 1944. Fortunately, the weather favored the Allies, and the attack took the Nazi forces by surprise. However, the battle of Normandy, called Operation Overlord, left high casualties on both sides.

"Families still share stories of loved ones lost during the war. However, it is remarkable to hear about a World War II pilot still living. Colonel Hamilton, the last surviving elite pathfinder pilot, was a memorable guest at the anniversary celebration.

"He told us about his trip over the English Channel and how it was his responsibility to drop off the courageous Pathfinders."

I continue my storytelling, and Mark leans toward me. "This is Hamilton's retelling of his experience with us. Hamilton told us how relieved he felt after he had delivered the primary American troops, the paratroopers, to occupied French soil early in the dark of morning. He completed half of his mission. However, he still had to fly back over enemy-controlled territory to England. That's when the trouble began. Hamilton's plane came under fire from German troops on the ground. He pushed the plane as fast as possible and hightailed it out of there at a low altitude. His copilot yelled at him to lift the right-wing or he was going to take off a French church's steeple."

"Whew, I'd say it's low altitude flying. That's pretty scary stuff," says Mark. "Did Colonel Hamilton ever sit in the cockpit of your DC-3 at any time during this flight?"

"Yes, we asked him if he wanted total control by flying a bit. We rearranged ourselves in the plane, released the control wheel to him, and I held my breath, hoping this ninety-seven-year-old pilot still had the strength and knowledge to fly."

"What happened next?" Mark questions.

"Well, Hamilton's face relaxed, and he enjoyed himself immensely. While he was flying, he explained about the Pathfinders and his passengers. They were the guys putting the markings ahead of time for the twenty-thousand parachuters due an hour later. These are our elite soldiers. A Pathfinder, whether you 'hit the silk' or are the one piloting the airplane, is a trailblazer—a high-risk job had to be done for the greater good. Flying the aircraft brought back all those memories for Hamilton.

"After flying briefly, Hamilton handed the controls back to Captain Sessions. He told us that war is a living hell, but you must follow orders. Our crew felt the historical significance of the moment and remained silent. Hamilton sat very still. He thanked us with tears in his eyes and moved out of the cockpit back to the passenger section. I sat next to him and asked him how the flying went for him this day—seventy-five years later. Hamilton said it didn't seem like that many years ago. He told us that trip in 2019 was better than his last time."

The solemn mood ends when Angelina and her dog come in. She says they're going for a walk and will return in thirty minutes.

"Oh, any more clues about your call this morning, Gramps?" she asks.

"Now that you mention it, the story I told Mark reminds me of something the caller shared. Can you believe they knew about John Sessions, the Historic Flight Museum, and the DC-3 we flew out of Spokane to Europe? The existence of the Historic Flight Museum is public knowledge, and so is our plane's history. You can look online for the reference number N877MG and read all about it. They did."

Betty checks her watch and looks at Mark. He sits on the edge of his chair, paying attention like a kid getting directions to a new Thrustmaster T-flight stick. "Okay, spill the beans on the aircraft, Eugene. You got control of this joystick," he says.

"Douglas Aircraft Company out of Long Beach built it the same year I was born, 1944. Their design included a long-range fuel tank and specialized engine for high altitude work going over The Hump."

"The Hump," Mark says, "refers to the Himalayan Mountains. I imagine we're talking 1944-45 and the revolution in China with the Shanghai exodus. A complex history few know about."

I smile at my cousin and say, "Betty, it's all online with the China-Burma-India operations. But I will tell you there is still a mystery about who blew up the plane's wing in Hong Kong. At the time, some fuzzy history, but the aircraft ended up back in the States, refurbished, and used as a VIP Super DC-3 for Johnson & Johnson. Time passes, equipment improves, and our DC-3 is rusty and tired. John Sessions comes to the rescue in 2006 and purchases it for his museum."

"Why?" Betty asks.

"Sessions collects and repairs planes made between 1927 and 1957. His collection spans the period from Charles Lindbergh's flight in 1927 and Boeing's 707, one of the premier commercial passenger jetliners in 1957. His passion and enthusiasm for aviation are outstanding. He has many folks who love to work on planes or fly them. His vintage planes are operational, starting with a 1939 Waco UPF-7."

"Why?" Betty asks again.

Mark and I nod our heads. We understand the why. Some of us are born to fly. It is in our blood.

Betty stands, preparing to head out. Simultaneously, the screen door opens, and Bijou has a tray of glasses and a pitcher of iced sun tea. She places the tray on a table and begins to fill the glasses.

"It's early. Stay for a glass of tea and enjoy the sweet story Gramps loves to tell. His story is calorie-free." Then Bijou turns to me and adds, "Gramps, the story prop for your sweet reenactment is on top of the laundry basket."

Chapter 20

I spot Sonny stretched out on the couch as I walk into the house to retrieve the visual aid for my storytelling. He takes up the entire sofa. It's difficult to recall him as the grandchild I used to lift into the cockpit of a small plane. He wanted to be a pilot like me at the time. Sonny described the job as "incredible." Just a few years back, Sonny took flying training, but his interests have switched, and he will not start a career in aviation.

He lifts his head up from the pillow and asks, "Hey, Gramps, we barbecuing those brats tonight?"

"Did you forget you ate them already? Let's all go out for dinner. You can meet the caller."

"No thanks, Gramps."

"Come on. It'll be a short conversation, and later we can feast together with no dishes or clean-up." I watch as he yawns, then checks his cell phone for messages. All the grandkids have a phone these days.

"Naw, you go without me."

His response leads me to suspect he knows more about the call. My grandchildren all make fun of me, saying I never know when to quit talking about aviation. Could they have arranged for one of their buddies to pull a practical joke on me? Sonny has to join me today.

I grab my prop for the story and return to the group outside. Sonny gets up from the sofa and follows me out to the deck.

"Keep your distance, or grab a mask," I say. Sonny only steps back and waits for my storytelling performance.

Unfolding the white linen square, I hold the handkerchief by the two corners. "A bit of background first," I say. "After World War II, there was the Cold War. The Berlin Blockade is said to have begun the war. Have you ever heard of the island of freedom?"

Betty shakes her head.

"How about West Berlin? Okay, the Berlin Wall was erected in 1961 and removed in November 1989. I'm talking about the same area, but before that, back in 1948."

"I'm getting the idea. The area is West Berlin but before the Wall," says Betty. She moves in closer to me to hear all of my story details.

"Correct, and Hitler's out of the picture, but the Soviet Union isn't. Germany was divided into four zones by the occupying Allies. The greedy Soviets cut off the land routes for West Berlin's food supply. No food—not even coal for fuel, and winter was coming. Stressful times, so Britain and America realized the population in West Berlin needed help." I hesitate, but the group remains attentive and waiting for my next words.

"The Brits and the USA came to the rescue. Our Air Force delivered tons of food and supplies to the airstrips. German women, working by hand, cleared off the bombed runways. It was a complicated time in post-World War II Germany. Volunteers by the tens of thousands helped solve the shortages." I whisper and beckon with my index finger to my audience. They lean in closer to listen.

Sonny is the exception.

"Here comes the sweet part. Colonel Gail 'Hal' Halvorsen, one of the transport pilots, made history happen. It started with him taking out two sticks of gum and handing them to a group of war-weary youngsters. The German kids surprised him by dividing it into several pieces for sharing. Next, they took turns smelling the wrapper and never asked for anything more."

I begin to twist the corners of the handkerchief in my hands as the others follow my motions in a hypnotic state. "Colonel Hal couldn't get the images of the smiles out of his head. So, now you know how the Candy Bomber got his idea."

"I've heard about him," says Mark. "Halvorsen flew the C-54, a cargo plane. I'm sure they also used it for the food, coal, and medical supplies." Betty gives her husband a thumbs-up signal.

"And a little extra special something," I add. "Colonel Hal tossed out his small candy-filled box. Soon, other airmen contributed their gum or candy to help the hungry kids in the blockaded city. Kids loved it, and it gave them hope and sugary happiness. The officers heard about his secret deed. They encouraged and supplied him for the rest of the year. So you see, two sticks of gum can make a big difference."

With perfect timing, I throw my crunched-up handkerchief high into the air. It billows open like a parachute. Attached to the corners of my makeshift parachute is a mini candy bar that Sonny snatches in mid-air.

"Handy to have height now," Sonny jokes. "I know Charles Lindbergh measured in at six feet three inches. Pity him in the Spirit of St. Louis's closed cockpit back in 1927."

"Okay, Sonny, enough. I'm the storyteller. So that grand finale with the confiscated candy, Mark, ends my 'sweet' story about the 70th Berlin Airlift anniversary we attended."

"When was this? Where was your plane? Were you already in Berlin?" Mark asks.

"The plane was in England, and the crew accepted the invitation and flew into Germany later in June 2019."

Sonny licks the chocolate from his fingers and adds, "Do you know about Colonel Halvorsen's nickname, Uncle Wiggle Wings?" He looks at me for the go-ahead signal. I nod.

Between bites of his prized candy bar, Sonny, the developing storyteller and salesman, continues, "I know how Halvorsen got the name of Uncle Wiggle Wings. He used the control stick, twisting it right and left, to dip the wings. Great use of the yoke manipulating the wings to say hello. Also, the German kids on the ground spotted which plane had the candy box."

"Roger that," I say. "So this same fellow, Colonel Hal, returned to Germany in 2019 for the event. He met hundreds of Germans ranging in age from five to ancient. The elder ones informed Halvorsen about getting sweets from the sky and sending him drawings so he could fly over their neighborhood. Operation Vittles lasted a year, with day and night supplies to West Berlin residents. It made a difference, and they were appreciative even after seventy years."

"How old is Colonel Halvorsen?" Betty asks.

"At the anniversary, our DC-3 had the honor of flying number two in the historical recreation of the airdrop. We didn't have a food cargo, but we did drop candy bags like the Candy Bomber. The cloudless blue sky filled with puffs of white miniature parachutes drifting toward the outstretched arms of the spectators was unforgettable. The roar of the plane's engine with the sight of the thousands of children permitted to dash onto the reserved airstrip was incredible. The best treat was that Colonel Halvorsen was there to see it all."

"Stop," Betty interrupts. "You didn't tell me. How old are these veterans? How old is Halvorsen?"

"He's ninety-eight years young."

"Yeesss!" Mark nods and gives his wife a fist bump.

"Gramps," Bijou adds, "I found his autobiography online and saw tons of print books about the Candy Bomber. So, you got to meet him, too? That is too sweet."

"Yes, I spoke with him about common interests like the Civil Air Defense service. Such a nice guy, so decent and humble. He told me he received a Congressional Gold Medal for his candy airdrop idea. He said all the fame and glory were nothing compared to the knowledge that his idea helped so many in a time of need."

The barking dog is the first thing we notice. Angelina emerges from behind the house. She joins us on the deck, pours herself a tea drink, and settles onto a chair. "I'm going to sit for a minute and relax. We had a good, long walk."

Lucy, the dog, on the other hand, is full of activity and sniffs everyone's shoes. Finally, she settles before me, stares me down, and barks twice.

"She heard parts of Gramps' dandy candy story." Angelina chuckles. "She craves a treat."

Horizontal "8"

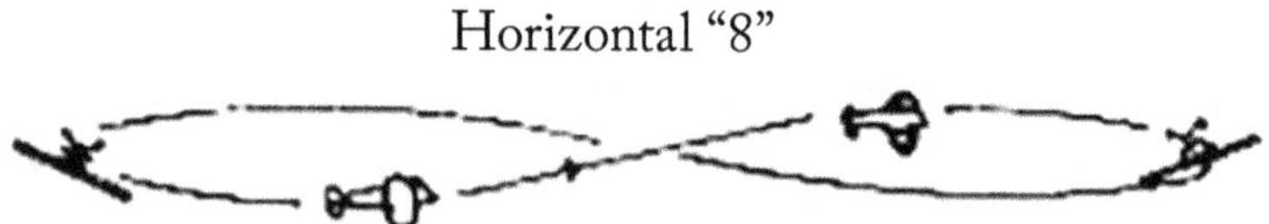

Chapter 21

With renewed energy, Angelina stands and announces she has goodies for us. She holds a filled ecofriendly, extra-thick, leakproof, lavender-scented dog poop bag.

"You're not pooping us?" asks Sonny.

She opens the bag for him and says, "Look closer. I picked these in the Oskar Cemetery. You can take them home with you, Betty. Who knew raspberries grew so well in a graveyard? Gramps, why are you looking so weird? They're only raspberries."

I do not know why, but a distant recollection of raspberries and graves pricks my memory.

As Betty reaches for the bag of raspberries, Mark glances at his watch, reminding her of the time. Betty agrees and says, "We must leave, but what a beautiful setting." She takes in the tree-lined view of the opposite shore as she turns. Her gaze follows the steady flow of water into Lake Superior, and she sighs and turns to stare again at the Wall of Fade. Her eyes devour the washed-out, sepia-toned family photographs. "Thank you for representing the family and our country during last summer's anniversary, Eugene. I'm sure you felt the spirit of all our departed relatives there with you. We'll try to pass on the Lucchesi storytelling skills to our children. It will require some practice."

Angelina offers her the newly picked, unwashed raspberries, and I see tiny scrapes on my granddaughter's arm. I draw her attention to them.

"Thorny stems," Angelina says. "Got my shoes dirty, too. Is there a problem, Gramps? You've got a strange look like you did this morning. Did you get another phone call?"

I ignore her.

Betty and Mark say their farewells to the three grandkids. "We enjoyed the visit, but I feel exhausted after all the years of traveling we covered in our conversations."

"Bless up, Betty," the girls say and give her and Mark air kisses.

I begin walking with them to their car. Mark waves me away as they proceed up the short incline. Betty starts to hum a song. A smattering of her words sparks a memory. I start humming along and singing a few words. I go inside, still singing from memory the chorus of, "I'll Fly Away."

"I recognize the song. It's classic rap," says Sonny.

"This song? It's an oldie from the thirties."

All three grandkids shout one word, "Wrong!"

Sonny shoves his mobile phone in my face and demands I watch a YouTube video performance. The song is new to me, but one part of the performance sounds familiar. The three kids are astonished when their gramps sings along a short segment with the well-known American rapper, actor, songwriter, and recording producer known as Puff Daddy.

"Not so fast," I say. "Tune into this classic gospel song." I locate the bygone tune on my phone's YouTube app. Twin sisters sing it, and their harmonizing voices sap my energy. This song is the 1950s version played at Caesar's funeral.

Sonny cranks up the volume on his modern take on the song. He starts a lively dance while plucking an air banjo. It returns me to reality. The yodel-like moans of the dog signal she enjoys our concert. The girls revolve around the room with arms flapping like bird wings. My emotions switch, and I cherish this simple moment of togetherness. I'm a lucky grandparent. We all laugh as the music ends.

"I get it, Gramps. We are all winners. The song is the same, but different," says Sonny. "And there's nothing different about me. I'm hungry. What's there to eat?" He moseys over to the refrigerator, flings the door open, and sorts the leftovers. The girls push him aside and rummage through the vegetable drawer, gathering greens and makings for a salad.

"Well, that certainly was a fun visit," I say to everyone as I walk back to the porch. "It was nice of Betty and Mark to be so interested in my stories. It was an honor to have had such a major part in D-Day 2019." I feel like I'm speaking to myself, yet Angelina comes beside me.

"There are too many cooks in the kitchen," she complains. We straighten out photos, and she wants me to tell her about my experiences in flight over the years.

"You want to know? In 1957 when Caesar died, airplanes were changing at warp speed. Uncle Fred flew from California to Chicago on a commercial jet for Caesar's funeral. Jet travel had arrived. You could fly faster, in more luxury and comfort than ever before. He probably came in on a DC-7, piston-driven engine because the DC-8 came out in 1958."

"Was it cheaper to fly then?" she asks.

"Nope, it was expensive to fly. About four or five times as much as today. Wages weren't as much either. Onboard flight safety could be hazardous to your health. A person could die by walking the interior aisle."

"You gotta explain," Angelina says.

"Well, some aircraft had glass partitions between first and second class. If the glass shattered, watch out for flying glass." I laugh at my pun. "Now, there were advantages like very little security. You could get to the airport thirty minutes before flight time and walk on because there wasn't any TSA check. I spoke to my buddy last night about the old days. He shared the story of flying up to Detroit Metro in their Beechcraft Musketeer. He landed and taxied his private

plane to the commercial twin-engine Convair's airstairs. After
bidding his mother, the passenger, farewell, she took her weekender
bag, disembarked his plane, and boarded her aircraft. There was no
security check. She took her assigned seat."

"I'd call it door-to-door service." We both chuckle.

"That's how it went in the fifties and sixties. Did you know they
used to hand out postcards on long hauls? A flight could get boring
without Internet access and movies. Still, you could always relax with
a cigarette, a cigar, or even a pipe. One could smoke in the plane, but
you dare not do it in a terminal or outside by the plane."

Sonny overhears this part of our conversation and chimes in, "I
know why. Fuel fumes." He comes closer to us and says, "Ka-boom!"
Between bites of his sandwich, he asks, "What was airplane food like
for the passengers then?"

"The meals were more elaborate, and real glassware and china
were used. And there were free alcoholic beverages."

"Sounds better than paying for the bad food now," Sonny says
and enjoys an additional bite of the sandwich.

"Another interesting fact deals with Black Americans as
passengers. Remember, I'm talking about the fifties and sixties, the
civil rights movement era. Almost all air travelers were white people.
There were remarkably few black passengers, but exceptions were
allowed if you were a musician or a sports personality and the airline
employee knew about you. There seems to be no defined policy."

"Not fair, not fair," protests Angelina. "I'm glad times have
changed."

"Caesar died in September 1957, precisely when the Little
Rock 9 made headline news. Remember the nine black students at
Central High School in Arkansas? It was the end of segregation and
the beginning of integration. President Eisenhower stepped in with
Federal troops to do the proper thing."

"Cheers to Ike. What can you tell me about African American aviators, Gramps?" asks Angelina.

"Malick, well, Emory Malick, is listed as our first Black pilot. Guess what year?"

"During World War II, the forties? I saw *Red Tails*, the movie about the Tuskegee airmen. Some real heroes never got proper recognition. Is Malick one of them?"

With a nod, I say, "Absolutely wrong. Malick and Caesar's aviation interests were similar. Please note Malick received his pilot's license in 1912. He beat Caesar by twenty years."

"How about an African American astronaut?"

I request a glass of water and receive one. I'm weary of chatting, and the meal looks delicious. My granddaughter's interest drives me on.

"Gramps, got a name and date for me? Remember, the astronaut?"

"I know he never endorsed Tang on any flight, but Astronaut Guion 'Guy' Bluford went up on the Challenger in 1983. He did four shuttle missions with NASA. Okay, enough of this. I'm hungry, too."

"One more question, Gramps," Angelina asks. "What's Tang?"

"What's for lunch?" I ask.

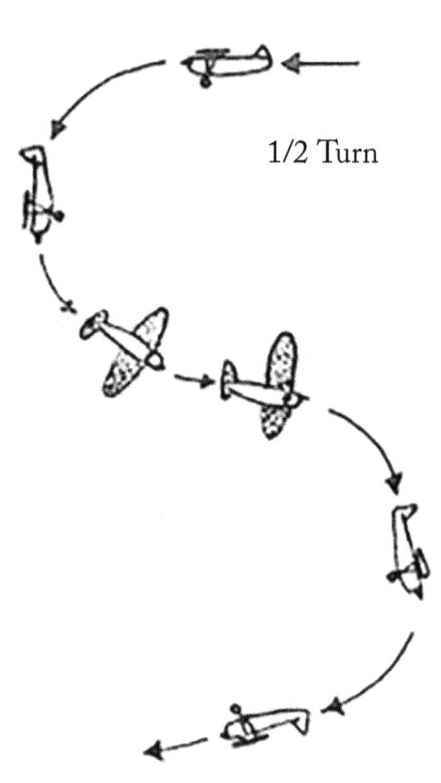
1/2 Turn

"Come and get it!" Bijou yells from the kitchen. We all gravitate toward the center island in the kitchen. My father hand-made the countertop from strips of teak. Years of use have not diminished the sheen he worked so hard to achieve when he built it.

The nails of the dog click on the floor as she darts around, hoping someone will give her a table scrap. "No begging, I fed you," says Angelina. "She always wants to eat, like you, Sonny."

"What will Karen be doing in Seattle today? How is her new grandson doing?" one of the kids asks.

Karen is my wife. We have been married for more than a decade and are both retired airline employees. I shout above the clatter in the kitchen. "She's spending time with him while I'm here with you. We're the modern blended family, and sometimes we need to share family times apart and together. We are both having a grand time with our grandkids."

"Right; it's always a grand time, Gramps," one of the kids replies.

Lunch is ready, and we all sit on a stool and grab items from the large platter with cheeses and cut meats. Bijou ladles out some homemade minestrone.

"*Stai zitto e mangia*," I say. "Your lunch is getting cold—be quiet; let's eat."

"Gramps, did the interviewer ask you anything about Karen's family? Is there a book or a movie about her father when he was a prisoner in World War II? I can see the title now—Lucky Captain Tom." Angelina, the creative cousin, asks.

"Nope, but there should be. It's an extraordinary story." As I continue eating, my mind replays the story of his lucky landing in

Sweden, a neutral country with the Flying Fortress, the B-17. He captained the plane safely to the ground with a crew of ten in their damaged B-17. Their other options were crashing in Germany or making a water landing in the ocean. The landing happened on May 8, 1944, another day to remember. They were fortunate indeed. Her father, Captain Tom, and crew spent time in the Swedish "prison." The jail was said to be a comfortable hotel room rather than an internment camp.

After my final slurp of soup, I recall a footnote to the war story. "You remember the large framed picture in our Seattle home? The one with photos and letters about the fifty veterans honored at the reunion in Sweden in 1987? It's difficult to imagine knowing the numerous soldiers who died throughout the war. Many servicemen continue to suffer from survivor guilt."

Bijou stands up and brings her dishes over to the dishpan. The window above the sink provides a clear view of the woods and cloudless blue sky. Gazing at the sky, she says, "Not all of Karen's family aviation history has a happy ending like the story of her father."

I know what happened that broke Karen's heart. Tommy, her younger brother, was a talented athlete, an Air Force Academy graduate, a stellar pilot flying secret missions in the Vietnam War, and a successful businessman—his life ended mysteriously.

His plane vanished from radar while flying a training session with the Southern California National Guard. There was no Mayday call, no radio contact—nothing. Years and decades have passed, and the tragedy remains a mystery. How can a family reconcile all of this? Tommy is no longer with us, but he is not forgotten.

Lunch is over, and everyone pitches in for clean-up. I have a lot of outside work to do before we close and depart tomorrow—no time to relax. Bijou calls pals on the East Coast while Angelina and Lucy go outdoors to play. Sonny appears to be preparing for a snooze on the living room sofa.

"How about helping me outside, Sonny? We can figure out where to go for dinner while we work. I'll treat for the meal, no clean up in the kitchen later."

"Dinner, sure, but I don't want to attend your meet-and-greet thing." Stretching his arms, he gets off the extra-long sofa and walks outside with me.

His mention of the meeting irritates me. Why does he keep bringing it up? Is he in on it and pulling my leg? He and his cousins will accompany me to meet this strange caller regardless.

We spend the next few hours working on the wooden dock, repairing weathered boards, and cleaning the yard. Michigan can be a winter wonderland, but mostly I wonder how people can tolerate it. I respect the older generations for their perseverance in living and staying in this region.

The mid-afternoon turns into late afternoon. Walking back into the house, I call for a quick family meeting. Unlike Caesar, I do not see myself as The Boss.

"Time for a mini-meeting. Gather round, okay. The first question is did you have anything to do with the joke call this morning?"

"Gramps, if we wanted to place a joke call, we'd have scripted it to be funnier. We would have asked if your refrigerator was running or if you had Prince Albert in a can. Something bizarre like that."

"Or say you had won the lottery. You know something unbelievable."

They all hee-haw with delight at their jokes. I don't crack a smile.

"Okay, end of the meeting," I tell them. "Time to start getting ready. You are coming with me. I don't want to hear n-o. I'm clearly stating it's a g-o for all of us. We leave in half an hour."

Sonny looks resigned and asks his usual question. "You're taking us out to eat afterward? What restaurant? I want to pick it."

"We can decide later," I say. "You can choose the restaurant after our mystery meeting is over." The girls start whining about how he always gets to pick. "That's enough—*basta*," I say in English and Italian.

Everyone scatters faster than cockroaches running from the light. Lucy dutifully follows Angelina around inside the house. Planning an outing makes the dog nervous.

The windows are shut and the doors closed. We are all set to leave. I look at my watch and realize we need to get aboard and depart now to reach our destination on time. "*Andiamo*; let's go," I remark, using my bilingual abilities. "Are you ready for takeoff?"

"Ready."

We leave the house and walk up the hill to my SUV outside the garage. Lucy comes wagging her tail, expecting to go. "We will fit in one car, but the dog must stay here."

Bijou asks Angelina, "Why didn't you name your dog Lindy instead of Lucy? You know, Lucky Lindy, the nickname for Lindbergh."

Angelina kisses Lucy goodbye and puts the dog into the garage. We hear her rummaging around to locate something for the dog. The dog whines, knowing she will be left behind. Angelina tells Lucy to enjoy the chewing time.

"I found a weathered shoe. Lucy won't get bored gnawing on the aged thing," she says. "Great-Grandma Norma sure saved everything. The shoe must be from the fifties. What sentimental reason can there be for saving a pair of scuffed shoes?"

There are no comments from the crew inside the car. Bijou is the first to speak. She places her hands over her eyes and begins, "I see a picture on the Wall of Fade. Great-grandma is a nine-year-old sitting on a timeworn upholstered footstool, and she's wearing a white dress with dark polka dots. Her short wavy hair is parted on one side. Her Mona Lisa-like smile is enchanting."

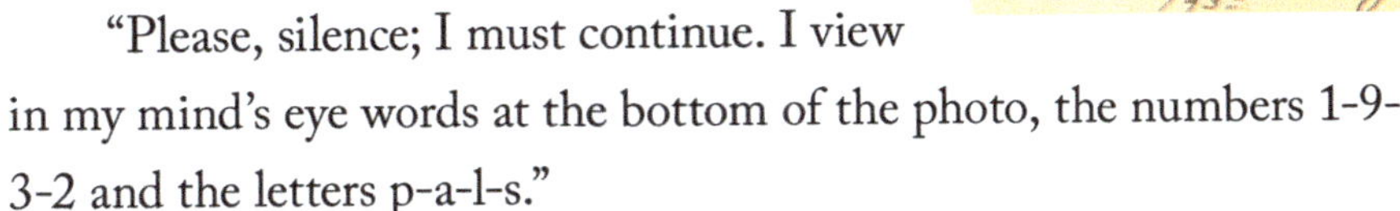

Groans erupt in the car. I wonder what Bijou had in mind? The mood begins to improve with her fun actions.

"Please, silence; I must continue. I view in my mind's eye words at the bottom of the photo, the numbers 1-9-3-2 and the letters p-a-l-s."

Again, moans are heard in the car. Bijou's crazy actions bring us together again as a family.

"Quiet, please; I need to finish. Yes, I understand. I now recognize the names. Norma and Lindy." Her eyes open as wide as the smile on her face. "Get it, Angelina?"

"Huh?"

"Lindy and Norma. Lindy is the dog she's hugging. Ever admire the RCA dog, Nipper? Norma's pet dog is black and white like Nipper. I bet Lindy's a fox terrier."

"Huh? Oh, never mind," says Angelina. "I hope my Lucy is happy chewing on that worn shoe."

A more comfortable silence fills the car. I'm beginning to wonder about Lucy's worn-out footwear. What made my mother save old shoes? Time will reveal everything, but now is the time to drive and focus on the road.

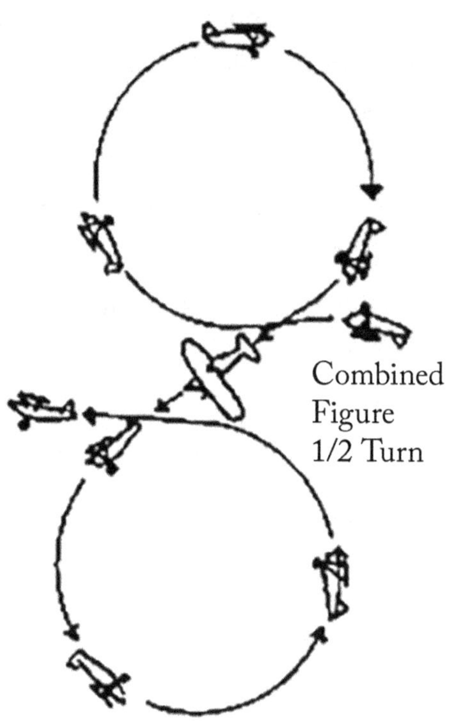

Combined
Figure
1/2 Turn

Chapter 23

As we drive along the canal, I check my rearview mirror and glance at the girl cousins. I see the family resemblance to some of their common ancestors even though the genes are diluted. As I notice Bijou leaning against the window and staring at the water, I think about the past. Angelina silently examines her nails and cuticles and reminds me of my mother. Sonny is sitting next to me with his eyes closed, pretending to be asleep, and I think about Nonno.

My mind returns to Lucy munching on the shoe. It puzzles me why people treasure old things. That is not my style. I'd rather throw something in the trash than save it.

After riding in silence for a while, I share my thoughts. "Great-Grandma Norma did save a lot," I say. "From shoes to letters. Can you believe I found my letter of employment from North Central inside the roll-top desk? It was dated May 1973."

"Did you know you always wanted to be a pilot, Gramps?" Bijou asks.

"Oh, I don't know. I always loved flying and the freedom of the sky. Maybe it's in the blood, my Lucchesi DNA. Or maybe I decided when I was a college student, at Tech, in the University Flying Club. You know they used the Sands airstrip next to Tech."

"You couldn't land a plane there now. The developers resurfaced the sand with topsoil and built houses," says Sonny. "Your letter from North Central was written in 1973. Wow, it's almost fifty years ago."

"After college, I started as a copilot with North Central. They merged and became Republic, and then Republic got purchased by Northwest Airlines and Delta Airlines. That covers over thirty years of commercial piloting. I flew everything from a DC-3 to a DC10-30. Spent three years as your Captain V. on the Boeing 747."

"Copilot to our captain," says Bijou. "No regrets, and you did it your way."

On cue, all three grandkids start to hum a well-known Frank Sinatra song.

Angelina adds some words of her own to the tune. As the volume of her voice increases in the car, all three join in the grand finale, "...you flew it your way." Laughter becomes a humming, and then a comfortable silence fills the car.

"I remember when I retired. It was my birthday, February 18, 2004. Your parents came to Hawaii and were passengers on the last leg of the flight into Minneapolis. You were too young to go, but their Grandma Norma greeted us at the terminal." I know their parents still discuss that last flight. I continue talking. "The passengers and crew couldn't believe the captain's eighty-one-year-old mother was at the gate as part of the welcoming committee."

Sonny adds, "You haven't stopped flying, only stopped getting paid for it, right? Any words of wisdom?"

"It's been the greatest ride. I enjoyed it all and hope the future will be as much fun. People usually look back and remember the good times. I'll ask you to look forward and make some fine memories," I say. "Those were my exact words from that retirement day as printed in the airline magazine."

"You're still in pretty good shape for a grandfather."

"I've been pacing myself throughout the years." It is still hard for me to act my age.

"How about any other unique flying memory, Gramps?"

My mind is racing; every flight you want to be routine, not unique, but I have an answer. "I flew over the Keweenaw Peninsula. It was a surprise flight for your great-great-grandmother, my Nonnie. We even got a photo and a write-up in the local paper. It was her birthday present, and she was eighty-two years young."

"I've got a question, Gramps. Did you ever want to be an astronaut?"

"No, Sonny, but I have the utmost respect for the elite group of ladies and men who make the cut, who put in the years of training and speak—"

"And speak Russian," Sonny cuts me off. "I thought about being an astronaut like John Glenn when I was young. He was older than you, Gramps when he flew the STS-95 on the Discovery. He did it at the young age of seventy-seven. And the youngest man, a Russian who got sick, was twenty-five."

"Impressive knowledge, but call them cosmonauts if they're Russian. Anything else you want to share, Sonny?" I am pleased my grandson has listened to me talk about aviation history.

"A little-known fact about life in space," Sonny continues. "It's dangerous to fart in space. The gas is flammable."

"Ick, that's sick," both the girls agree.

"But he's correct," I say. "Burping and crying in a gravity-free environment can be an issue. Scientists study and analyze stuff. Astronauts are human." I am wondering now where Sonny picked up this fact.

"Double ick!"

Working as a docent at the Museum of Flight contributes to my knowledge and fascination with space. It is hard to believe Apollo 13's fiftieth-anniversary events took place months ago. Jim Lovell is my favorite spaceman alive. Humble, intelligent, and ninety-two years old. I wish Caesar could have met him. Aviation pioneer meets space pioneer. Their conversation would have been out of this world.

I'm just a plain airline pilot with many miles who can't keep up with the latest space missions. Forget about the neighboring moon. Scientists are making Mars and beyond a reality. With the private rivalry for space exploration, things are changing quickly.

"I'm getting hungry," says Sonny. "Can we chow down first and go on your secret interview event later?"

The girls begin to bicker about their choice of restaurants. I know where I want to go. However, my recommendation will not count, and I did promise the kids could choose tonight.

"No, you won't starve in the next hour."

Sonny struggles to get something out of his back pocket. With one hand, he starts to check out restaurant listings. He grumbles, "Poor reception here. Are we almost there?"

After a few traffic lights, we come to Michigan Tech University's Sherman Field. I cheer, "Go, Huskies," as a faithful alumni.

I spot daisy clusters blooming near the football field. The wildflowers' yellow petals and black centers complement the Tech school colors of black and gold. However, the blooms remind me of the old South Range garden. Passing the athletic field, I spot the Forest Hill Cemetery ahead.

As I round the next corner toward the prearranged meeting spot, the sun shines directly into my eyes, blinding me for a split second.

"Stop! "You're going to hit the dog, Gramps."

Chapter 24

Fortunately, my reaction time is swift, and I miss the little dog. Defensively I remark, "What's a beagle doing running around here? Was it chasing an animal?"

"Oh, it looks like Snoopy. I love those dogs," says Angelina. "I wonder where the owner is? Do you imagine it's lost? I'm glad you stopped in time. The dog is waiting for us to come and pet him."

Moving my car a few yards, I park off the dirt road by the designated spot. I doubt any vehicles will be passing by in this memorial park. The kids get out of the car and walk toward the dog. Turning off the engine, I get out, too. The small beagle, a popular hunting dog in the Keweenaw Peninsula, remains standing in place, wagging its tail like a pendulum on a grandfather clock.

"Apollo, come," a girlish voice from behind me commands. The dog obeys faster than my kids ever did. My three grandkids face the dog owner, and the girls wave a welcome hello. Turning around, I spot two figures heading our way.

The taller person is wearing a long-sleeved black, airy chiffon full-skirted dress with black shoes and tights. Her long dark ponytail sways right and left with her every step. The dress billows around her like a dark dust cloud as she moves. She looks younger than my granddaughters. The younger one wears camouflage sweatpants and an enormous sweatshirt. The outfit melts into the semi-forested backdrop. These youngsters do not look like tourists or locals. Their dress and confidence is—different.

"Are you lost?" I ask. "Where are your parents? Why are you out here alone?"

"To meet you," the girl replies.

Her mysterious appearance, clothing, youthfulness, and attitude surprise me. We all stand fixed in position as she comes closer to us. The smaller kid might be a relative, or perhaps, the older one is the babysitter. My eyes widen with surprise as she appears to glide closer and closer to me.

Then she speaks. "Hello, Captain Vezzetti. I assume these are your three grandchildren. Hello, Angelina, Bijou, and Sonny."

My grandkids move and create a semi-circle with this strange girl and myself in the center. The little guy remains standing behind her at a safe distance, and the Snoopy-like dog sits on the dirt at her feet.

"Gramps," Bijou says, "I bet she's the person on the phone. It's your interviewer. It's not a prank."

I stay wary, fearful that a TV film crew will emerge from behind one of the bushes and reply, "Well, I assume it's true, or is there a surprise in store?" The unknown girl smiles like the Mona Lisa.

Angelina starts petting Apollo, the dog, and Bijou asks the girl about her dress. In response, the girl giggles and does a 360-degree twirl. Her fancy dress twists around her like a protective circle. Sonny walks over to read a patch on the sleeve of the little guy.

For some reason, a shiver runs along my spine and goosebumps make my hair stand up. The scene makes me feel very uncomfortable. Why did I pretend meeting here was a sane idea? The mysterious girl and my granddaughters are in a deep conversation. I pick up words from their discussion that begins to tie loose ends together. Angelina motions for me to join the group. Now I associate the voice on the phone with this girl's.

"Gramps, you're not going to believe this. Listen to this family's story. They know about our Great-Great-Grandfather Caesar, and they know about the Sands airfield. They have a family home nearby."

Bijou interrupts her cousin, just as excited, and adds more details. "This girl's great-grandfather worked for your grandfather at the Sands."

"Wait, let's start from the beginning. Tell me your name again; I never got it correct this morning when we talked. The call was unusual. I need to know…" I begin to ask.

Angelina butts into the conversation. "Wow, her grandmother was your age when your Grandfather Caesar died. She went to his funeral back in 1957. Don't you remember the family? Can you believe it, Gramps?"

"No, this is all too much. I somehow can't believe it."

We all stare at the bright-eyed girl. She turns around, hears a whistle, and waves at an older person in the distance. I'm happy to know the kids are not alone in this place. It's reassuring to see another adult.

Things are moving too quickly for me. "Do you mind?" I say to the girl. "I have some questions." Her ponytail swings up and down.

"May we begin with your name?"

"I'm Florence Terran, and this is my brother, Franklin Terran. You can remember my name by saying Florence Nightingale, but never call me Florence. You're a pilot. You know about airflow, so please call me Flo. You know I can be turbulent or laminar."

Angelina whispers in my ear, "What does laminar mean?"

Flo's brother says, "What she means is sometimes she's calm, like a laminar airflow, and sometimes she's chaotic, like air turbulence you feel in a plane." The boy continues to talk. "And please call me Frank. It's a name we love to keep in the family. Our great-grandfather worked at the Sands and was Caesar's airplane mechanic. He knew and loved your grandfather, Captain Vezzetti."

I need a genealogical flow chart to keep track of everything. I approach Flo and introduce myself. The details of our phone chat are starting to come together and make sense. I am taking it seriously now.

"Flo, I'm happy to meet you and glad you explained the history of our two families. I never knew any of this. So the man I met at the Sands on the day of Caesar's funeral back in 1957 was your great-grandfather Frank?"

"Correct. Of course, I never met him. He was way before my time. I'm thirteen years old, and my little brother is eight. But I will be fourteen soon, and I know aviation is in my blood."

"That explains why you chose and phoned me."

"But he wasn't your only pick for the interview," pipes in her brother. "You had his D-Day anniversary boss on the list, John Sessions. He owns the DC-3 and all the planes at the Historic Flight Museum in Washington. Everyone in the family voted on who she should interview."

She placed a finger over her lips to silence him. I chuckle and add, "Flo, John Sessions, and his patriotic aviation family are worthy subjects. Besides, he was the official captain of our 2019 anniversary event. His brother joined us, too. I'm honored to be in the same company."

My grandkids team up and face Flo and her brother, and they begin to play twenty-one questions.

"Flo, did you know that the father of Sessions was a sergeant in the US Army and parachuted behind enemy lines in World War II? Did you know they presented him with a Purple Heart?" Sonny starts the game.

Angelina does not miss a beat and asks, "Did you know, Flo, his brother, Michael, the Smokejumper, parachuted into forest fires? Can you believe he later became a training contractor for the Army Special Forces, the Green Berets?"

"Did you know John Sessions crashed his biplane with four passengers and severed his left foot?" Bijou follows up with a final question.

Flo swishes her ponytail up and down. She answers yes to all the questions. "I also know he reported the wind shear dropped him about fifty feet during his take-off in Vancouver. The accident happened about two years ago now. Sessions got all the passengers to safety. There were no deaths due to the 'bit of a bang,' Sessions reported. He didn't want the accident to change his life. His partial leg amputation didn't slow him down. Three months later, he's the proud owner of a new prosthetic Cheetah Blade Flex-Foot, which handled the plane brakes just fine."

She stops to take a breath, straightens out her skirt, and grins. "But I selected you, Captain Vezzetti, because of our family ties. It dates back to the Sands airfield, the kindness the Lucchesi family shared with our family, the fact you're a Michigan Tech graduate and a famous local aviator."

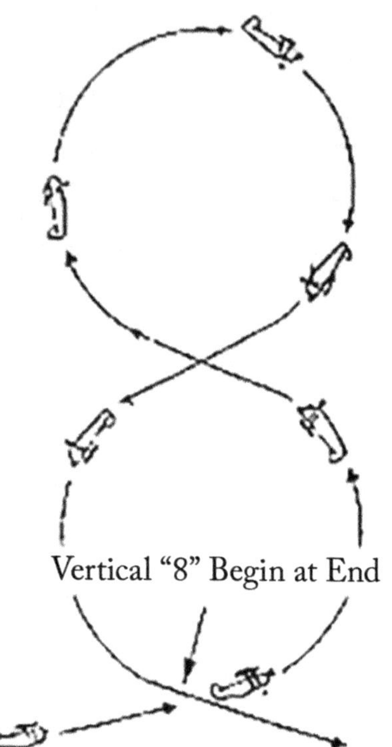

Vertical "8" Begin at End

Chapter 25

A soft bark is heard from Apollo as he dashes between Flo and the person approaching us on the road. An older woman gestures to the children and pats Apollo on the head. Hidden under a scarf knotted under her chin is her long gray hair. Her brown sweater and skirt are old and worn. The brown loafers on her feet are sensible footwear. In contrast to her understated style, she carries a glittery sequined backpack. I study her pleasant face but do not recognize her.

"Hello, everybody. I'm Flo and Frank's *babushka*, their Grandmother Nadia," she says in a friendly way. "I'm so glad you all could meet one another here. And I'm so pleased Flo chose you, Captain Vezzetti, as her subject." Looking at Flo, she continues, "The gift we've selected is perfect." The boy and Flo move closer to their grandmother, and she hands the flashy backpack to Flo.

Looking at me, she says, "Did Flo tell you I attended the funeral services for Caesar back in 1957? You and I are the same age, and I can still picture you dashing through the crowd after you spotted the plane in the sky. I told my mother you went to the Sands."

"It's unbelievable," I say.

"My father, Frank, told me about the conversation you two shared back in '57. It kicked off a discussion at home about dying. Before Caesar's funeral, my mother had never talked about her bad war memories. She opened up more about her life in Russia after it. Your adventure to the Sands helped us understand grief and death over the years. When I remember those around here, I tend to smile."

She extends her arms, and we all know she's referring to those buried in this cemetery. "Flo asked me to join you here in the Forest Hill Cemetery. She felt it would have lots of meaning for you. Besides, our home is nearby, and it was convenient for us."

"Tell him about the shoes we've saved all these years, Grandma," says her grandson Frank.

"What about the Sho-Luks?" I am amazed at how swiftly the words escape my tongue. I had no idea what had happened to the shoes Nonno and I had bought together, and I am equally astounded that I recall their name.

"A short time after your grandfather's funeral, your Uncle Geno came to the Sands with a box. Inside were Caesar's new shoes. He handed them to my father. He asked Frank to keep the shoes and wear them. It would be a shame not to use the fancy Sho-Luks, Geno said."

Again, I murmur the word, "Unbelievable."

"My father felt fortunate to receive them. He never wore them, but he put them on a shelf and always talked about filling those shoes by being a decent person and fine aviator—like Caesar Lucchesi. It worked, and our family's history has always involved aircraft or aviation."

Frank steps closer to his sister and points to her backpack. "Show him the picture Great-Grandfather Frank took at the Cleveland Air Race in 1932, our special one with Amelia Earhart."

Flo opens her backpack and removes a framed photograph. It reminds me of one we have on the Wall of Fade. People are startled to see a famous female aviator in the picture.

"Wow!" screams everyone at once.

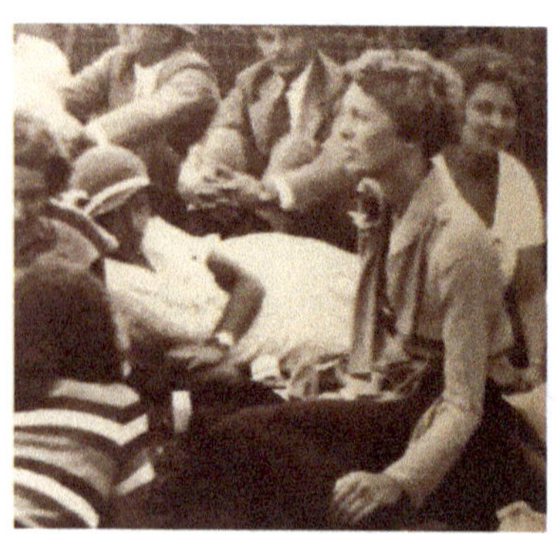

Amelia is sitting on the ground surrounded by Powder Puff aviatrixes in the picture. But it also includes my grandparents standing, talking, and watching the group. Frank, the mechanic, must have taken this rare picture with them at the air show while standing opposite the Lucchesi group.

"Here, it's for you." She hands it to me. "We made a copy and framed it to thank you for being a great subject to research and interview."

I am speechless and stand there with my mouth open.

"Say thank you, Gramps," says Bijou.

Angelina answers for me. "We accept with honor, and it will join our historical photo collection."

My three grandchildren look at me with new admiration and understanding. Apollo circles the group and begins to bark.

"Okay, Apollo," Grandmother Nadia says. "He wants to make sure you ask Flo a question about her plans for the future. You'll see we named the dog Apollo for a reason."

Recovering my composure, I respond, "Okay, Flo, your turn. Tell me about your future aviation plans. Do you want to be a pilot like me?" I'm thrilled she has placed me on a pedestal as a great example.

"No, sir, I intend to be an astronaut. I told you that during our interview call."

"I'm starting to make sense of all of this. Yes, you did mention that, and it's terrific. Good for you, Flo. I'm sure you'll be an outstanding astronaut. I'm proud to know you. And…" bending to pat the dog's head, I add, "Apollo always reminds you of your plans."

Her brother speaks and raises his arm to show the lettering stenciled on the sleeve. The stylized letters N-A-S-A are visible along with the words Space Mission 2.0 in red. He adds, "Flo will do it, too. Our mom works in MARC, the aerospace engineering research center at Michigan Tech. Have you ever heard of Professor Terran? She's my mom. But I will be a mechanic, like my relative who was your grandfather's mechanic."

"That's super, Frank. I have no doubt both of your dreams will come true. It has been unbelievable meeting you and learning about your family, Flo," I say. "Call anytime with a question, and we can arrange a time to meet. Will you promise me a copy of your final paper, Flo? I am extremely honored you chose me for your subject."

We exchange farewells, and I again thank them for the picture. Flo's grandmother AirDrops their contact information on my cell phone.

"Where is your house?"

She points in the direction along the road off of the cemetery woods. "Come on, kiddies; it's time to head home. It's getting to be suppertime."

Brother and sister grasp each other's hands. Little Frank turns for a final wave. We all wave back, smiling as the trio departs.

The stillness in the cemetery surrounds us as we gaze at a tombstone. It's a granite stone with the word Lucchesi engraved on it. Sonny is first to notice the faint sound.

"What's that noise? Is it a plane?"

My eyes close to concentrate. I guess it to be a single rep engine or a Piper Cub. No, perhaps it's a Cessna. Like a bolt of lightning, I flash back to standing at this same spot in 1957, hearing the purr of a plane overhead.

Opening my eyes, I move to gather my grandchildren into my arms. The kids giggle but love the closeness. Then I point to the burial plot. All eyes focus on the monument with the family name etched into the granite. "Think of your relatives who are buried here and smile. Remembering them is the way to keep loved ones with you." I picture Uncle Geno sitting at a piano and the Lucchesi family around a kitchen table, sharing family lore. I raise my hand to cover my mouth, and I bite my lip. Tears blur my vision.

"I understand the look. It's good to talk about it, Gramps?" says Angelina.

"You know I love you, but I need to tell you. Don't ever take anyone for granted. Things can change in an instant, as they did for me. It switched the night Nonno died. I told him good night. But I never said farewell. I regret it."

Sonny looks directly into my eyes. "You were only thirteen. Forgive yourself," he wisely says. "Grieving is the high price you pay for love. It's okay, Gramps."

"Don't waste your time worrying about a wrong decision years ago. You've had quite a day. We are very proud of you. And we love you, Gramps," Bijou adds and gives me a peck on the cheek.

"Thanks, kids. I believe being prepared for opportunities is part of the Lucchesi legacy. I hope you take it to heart. We're fortunate indeed." With a final hug, the four of us separate. I blink skyward and cannot believe what is happening.

Sonny confirms it. "Hey, look; do you see what I see? Someone in the plane is doing a wing wave over the cemetery."

"What a perfect way to say goodbye to this place. Let's go. It's time to eat. Life is for the living, and we need to refuel. Please, not too much arguing over choosing a restaurant. I don't want to start with indigestion."

And with those words, we tumble into our car. The grandkids whisper a secret plan of their own. Sonny announces with a grand gesture, "Gramps, we have decided to treat you to dinner tonight." They add in unison, "It's your choice!"

Discussion Questions from the Author

Now that you've read this book, I hope you'll think about some of the concepts it contains. My interest in aviation history and historic aviators, as well as my writing on the theme, suited my academic side. I also believed it was critical to include dealing with sadness in the plot. The worldwide epidemic may or may not have directly influenced your family, but now we are still affected in degrees. May you and your loved ones have a long and healthy life.

Below are some questions that may serve as a springboard for a more in-depth conversation with a child, an elderly loved one, or your inner Jiminy Cricket.

1. What were your thoughts about thirteen-year-old Eugene's actions at the cemetery? What would you have done in Eugene's or his parents' shoes?

2. How did Eugene benefit from the airstrip mechanic's advice to remember and smile? What phrases would you have used?

3. Did Cousin Carolyn and Eugene's explanations of life and death make sense to you? What words would you choose to express your emotions?

4. Which of the cousins' "remembering" ideas did you like the most? What have you done or could you do to honor a loved one?

5. How did Eugene's family assist him as a child and eventually in adulthood? How do you go about getting emotional help and support?

Acknowledgments

I am grateful to everyone who helped make this book possible, starting with my brother, Eugene Vezzetti. His personal flying experience and docent training at the Museum of Flight provided me with accurate aviation timelines and information. Grazie to the members of the Lucchesi and Vezzetti families whose shared storytelling sessions recounting tales of yore resulted in informative and humorous material as well as great reunions. I appreciate John Sessions' enthusiasm for aviation and for allowing me to present his stories and adventures. Karen Fishburn Vezzetti deserves praise for her contributions to the book by permitting me to share her family's patriotic service. Scott O'Brien, Robert Myers, Don Moore, Jim Harwood, and Jackie Kahn gave valuable aircraft and flying advice and tidbits. I have used many of their ideas in the book. Linda Silas and Lorraine Perry are commended for their professional insights into how children deal with death, grief, and remembrance.

Also, I thank the students, teachers, and friends who were alpha and beta readers for their first readings and invaluable input. And to my good-natured, brutal editor, Lou Ellyn Helman, I'm glad you discovered you are part Italian and better understand how I think. Kudos to Superior Book Productions in helping create a superior manuscript.

Finally, a heartfelt thank you to David, my husband, for his support.

About the Author

Maria Vezzetti Matson is an individual with tenacity. Born in Michigan's Upper Peninsula, she grew up with a rich Italian heritage from her immigrant grandparents that would eventually inspire her to write.

Maria attended the same grade school and high school as her mother in the Adams Township School District in the Copper Country. Her undergraduate teaching degree is from Northland College, Ashland, Wisconsin. Years later, she earned a Master of Education from Loyola-Marymount University in Los Angeles, California.

Before her teaching career in California, Maria worked for a major airline on the ground, but like her Italian ancestors, flying is in her blood. Connecting and visiting relatives in Italy's Tuscany and Piedmont regions is one of her favorite travel destinations.

During her teaching career, Matson remained with the Hawthorne Public Schools in Los Angeles Country for thirty years. She has experience in grades K-8.

In 2011, Maria published her first book, *Gelsomina's Story of Caesar Lucchesi*, a memoir of her Italian-American grandparents. That could have been the end of her publications, but an author friend encouraged Matson to begin her next story. She now has four books in print—two more about her family—*Alone to America* about her grandmother's journey to the United States from Italy in 1902 and *Legacy of an Immigrant* about her family's role as aviation pioneers—and her physics fiction coloring activity book, *Journey into the Land of Hues.*

Today, Maria splits her time between her native Upper Michigan and Northern California. She is enjoying retirement and spends her spare time entertaining visiting guests in Sonoma's wine country, traveling to the East Coast to visit grandchildren, playing golf, and taking trips abroad. Her husband, David, encourages her to fish, exercise, and prepare homemade meals.

Maria's vlog, *The Zia Mia*, portrays her Italian side. She wants her writing to entertain and inform generations of readers. Visit her website: MariaVezzettiMatsonAuthor.com.

More Books by Maria

If you enjoyed *Legacy of an Immigrant*, be sure not to miss Maria Matson's other books.

Gelsomina's Story of Caesar Lucchesi

Let Jennie, Gelsomina's American name, share her life's story with you as an immigrant, new bride, mother, and family business owner from the early 1900s to the late 1950s. Based on actual events of the Lucchesi family in the Upper Peninsula of Michigan.

Alone to America

Matson's love for sharing history continues in this story of her maternal grandmother's solo journey in 1902 from Italy to the United States. Alone to America is a timeless tale. The saga of immigration to a new country may resonate with your own family's history.

Journey into the Land of Hues

Do you ever wonder what life would be like in a world of darkness? Would a desire to learn about the secret of the spectrum motivate you to be curious and courageous? Let Roloc, the Ot, take you on an imaginary trip into the world of hues. A coloring activity adventure for all ages.

Visit the author's website at:
MariaVezzettiMatsonAuthor.com

9 780983 199052